TREACHERY IN DISGUISE

"We have the assistance of human scientists," said Dr. Morrow.

"Excellent. You managed that even after our fleet was forced to leave Earth. That is remarkable. How did you manage to enlist their aid?"

"Shall we say they are not in a position to turn us down?" He smiled. A most convincing human expression, Medea thought.

With Morrow and his minions working for her back on Earth, it wouldn't be long before she would be ready to attack the humans once again. They had been beaten the first time by a resistance force—and some very bad luck. Now Medea had a resistance of her own working on Earth.

She rose and stretched her leathery limbs. Discipline on the ship was getting too lax, she thought. She would see to it that everyone wore their human disguises while on duty.

They would wear them until Earth was under her power . . .

THE FLORIDA PROJECT

Tim Sullivan

PINNACLE BOOKS **NEW YORK**

This novel is a work of fiction. Names, characters, places, and incidents are either the product of the author's imagination or are used fictitiously. Any resemblance to actual events or places or persons, living or dead, is entirely coincidental.

V: THE FLORIDA PROJECT

Copyright © 1985 by Warner Bros., Inc.

An original Pinnacle Books edition, published for the first time anywhere.

First printing/February 1985

ISBN: 0-523-42430-2

Can. ISBN: 0-523-43418-9

Printed in the United States of America

PINNACLE BOOKS, INC.
1430 Broadway
New York, New York 10018

9   8   7   6   5   4   3   2   1

To Nana and Dad, who loved to read,
and to Dad and Charlie, who loved adventure

ACKNOWLEDGMENTS

Thanks to Somtow Sucharitkul, Bob Collins, and Sharon and Bryan Webb, beloved friends; to Phil and Jan Cox, for their invaluable research; and to Harriet McDougal, editor and friend.

Special thanks to the courageous staff of the Columbia Pike Branch Library in Arlington, Virginia, who helped, whether they knew it or not.

And finally, to Michael and Marion Dirda, who provided a quiet haven for me to write this book; and to their son Christopher, born wearing a propeller beanie midway through *The Florida Project*'s gestation period.

V:
THE FLORIDA PROJECT

Chapter 1

A thick fog hung over the swamp. Vague shapes rose out of the mist as the canoe moved toward them. Billy Tiger, plying his oar through the still water, recognized them for what they were: cycads, cypress trees, banyans, palmetto clumps. After all, he had grown up in the Everglades, even if he had been away a couple of years.

The morning silence was belied by a sinuous ripple just under the water's surface.

Billy let the canoe glide to a stop near a banyan tree. He dropped his fishing line over the side and leaned back, pushing his Stetson over his eyes. The sun was just coming up, and it was very peaceful. He welcomed the opportunity to just drift and let his mind wander for a change, without thinking about his girlfriend Marie or his older brother John bugging him about one thing or another. John in particular harped on Billy's leaving college after only two years. Everybody on the Seminole reservation had expected great things from him, and John had sacrificed a lot to get Billy into school after their parents died. But things just hadn't worked out at the university, and ever since he'd come home, Marie had been talking about getting married. With only half a college education and not a penny to his name, Billy didn't consider himself the best prospect in the world. But he did love Marie, and she continually assured him that was all that really mattered.

"Hey," he said to himself, his voice reverberating through the swamp, "I thought you were gonna go fishing, not soul searching."

He heard a flamingo's screech in the distance. Scared by a 'gator? He heard splashing too, but it sounded as if the big reptiles were taking to water to hide, not to hunt.

Billy felt a tug on his fishing line.

"All *right*," he said, allowing the fish to swim out a little, playing him, waiting for the right moment to haul him in. For a few seconds Billy thought he'd lost him. He didn't feel the fish moving at all, but he sat tight, knowing that they sometimes doubled back under the boat. Billy peered into the murky water, smelling the rich, decaying odor of the swamp.

Suddenly the line jerked spasmodically. The fish was fighting for all he was worth. Twenty yards from the canoe, there was a splash and the gleam of a silver back. Billy began to reel him in.

Just as he pulled the struggling fish out of the water, he heard a low hum. A boat? He didn't have time to think about it as he dropped the flopping fish in the canoe.

Billy was momentarily blinded by a flash of blue. When he could see again, the water next to his canoe was boiling. Another blue flash and then another sizzled the water around him. An energy bolt struck a banyan tree, blasting off a limb in a shower of sparks and a billow of smoke. The limb splashed into the water, rocking the canoe in its wake.

A shadow passed over him. Billy looked up and saw silver disks gliding around a cypress tree with men clad in red uniforms riding them. They all wore sunglasses and—their faces were green.

No, not men. Visitors.

It couldn't be. The Visitors had been driven away. There was a toxin in Earth's ecosystem that should have killed them all. But the acrid smell of smoke told him what he saw was so.

A blue laser beam whooshed by his head, convincing Billy that whatever he may have heard, these were definitely Visitors attacking him.

He reached for the shotgun hidden under his backpack on the canoe seat. Drawing and cocking at the same time, he glanced up to see a Visitor swooping down at him, weapon at the ready.

Billy fired, and the Visitor flew backward off his antigravity disk, slamming into the banyan and sliding down into the water. The disk wobbled and turned on its side, knifing neatly into the water. Billy let a second Visitor have it with the double barrel's second round, but there were so many of them now he had to choke back his fear as he plunged his fingers desperately into the backpack in search of more shells.

Whump. The prow exploded in a burst of flame, and the canoe overturned. Everything went into the water: the shotgun, the backpack, the fish, the gear and tackle, the Stetson, and Billy.

He swam underwater as far as he could, reaching the submerged roots of the banyan tree and pulling himself around the back of the swamp giant. When he couldn't hold his breath any longer, he bobbed to the surface.

Three lasers were pointed straight at him.

Billy shut his eyes tight and prayed, but the searing heat he expected never came. Instead, two of the disks descended, one on either side of him. From the third, the forked tongue of an alien darted as it spoke.

"We don't want to kill you," the lizard man's rasping voice said. "If we had wished to kill you, we would have done so before you ever saw us."

"What do you want?" Billy demanded.

The green, scaly face twisted into an expression that might almost have been a smile. "We only want you to come with us."

"Do I have any choice?"

"No."

The two Visitors knelt on their antigravity platforms and

pulled their weapon straps over their shoulders. Their clawlike hands free, they reached into the water and pulled the gasping Billy out by his armpits.

"Why are you doing this?" Billy screamed. Water streamed from his clothing, and his black hair hung limply in his eyes. "What are you gonna do to me?"

The Visitor who had spoken didn't answer this time. Instead, he turned on his antigravity disk and began to lead the way through the swamp.

Billy was about to try to wrest himself free of the two who were carrying him, but he saw the water below turn to white foam. 'Gator tails thrashed as the bodies of the two Visitors he had shot were pulled under.

He had no choice. Soaking wet and dangling from between two disks, he resigned himself to his abduction—and prayed there would be a way to escape later.

Chapter 2

Turning into the asphalt parking lot of Nutech, Inc., Jack Stern steered his 1985 Datsun 280-ZX into a parking space. There were already quite a few cars in the lot, and people dressed in tuxedos and gowns were getting out of vehicles and walking toward the monolithic buildings, new and pristine shapes rising out of manicured lawns. Sprinklers just out of range of the walk hurled miniature rainbows against the Florida sun.

Inside the nearest building, Jack found himself in a milling crowd. The lobby was like a terrarium, with all sorts of trees and flowers under glass. Jack liked it, but he was too preoccupied to enjoy the pleasant sights and smells. He wondered where Sabrina could be. She should have met him right here, but there wasn't any sign of her. A lovely girl brought a tray with tiny sandwiches on it, crusts neatly trimmed from the bread. Jack was hungry after driving all the way from Miami up the coast, so he grabbed one.

"Aren't you Jack Stern?"

Jack turned to see a balding, middle-aged man with a deep suntan.

"Yes, I am."

"Maybe you could give me an autograph," the man said in a jovial voice. "I should probably tell you it's for my kid, but it's really for me, so why lie about it. I'm a big football fan."

Jack politely signed a napkin for him, and the man engaged him in conversation. He was an investor in Nutech and was originally from New York. He didn't know Sabrina.

"I hope the Dolphins make it to the Superbowl this year," the man, whose name had already slipped Jack's mind, said. "What brings you to Nutech anyway, Jack?"

"I have a friend who's going to be employed here as soon as the laboratories open next week. The lady I mentioned—Sabrina Fontaine."

"Oh? What does she do?"

Jack smiled. "She's a biogeneticist."

"Wonderful," the football fan said. "I have to tell you, though, that I don't know a thing about all this." He winked as he gestured at the building around them. "Except that all the market analysts say there's a fortune in it."

As the football fan rambled on, Jack heard someone call his name, a female voice. He looked around the crowded lobby, expecting to see Sabrina.

Instead, he saw one of the serving girls walking toward him. "Mr. Stern," she said, smiling prettily. "I recognized you from TV. There's a message for you here."

She handed him a folded slip of paper, and Jack opened it as he thanked her and excused himself from the company of the man who had been talking his ear off.

The message was short and sweet. It was from Sabrina, and it said that she couldn't come to Nutech's dedication ceremony.

Great, Jack thought, she's going to be working here and she doesn't show up—and after I drove all the way from Miami.

There was more. Jack felt a tightening in his chest as the note explained that she wasn't going to take the position with Nutech after all. She had been offered a job with another firm, and it promised to be the most exciting work she would ever find. She couldn't discuss it now, and she would be out of town for a few days, but she would be in touch. Love, Sabrina.

Jack felt awkward and embarrassed standing around with all these businessmen and scientists, knowing that Sabrina wasn't coming. He loosened his tie and started toward the building's main entrance. This new job Sabrina was taking must really be something for her to stand him up like this. He trusted her, of course, but she would have some explaining to do when he saw her next or spoke to her on the phone.

When he saw her next. When would that be? Jack felt a pain in the pit of his stomach. This was all wrong. Not that he doubted it was her handwriting or anything like that. But, dammit, it just wasn't like her to do this.

"Aren't you a flanker for the Dolphins?" a young woman asked as Jack unlocked the car door. He absently signed an autograph for her and then got in. The upholstery and steering wheel were hot as hell as he started up the engine.

Driving toward the interstate, Jack had a hunch that something was going to happen, and it wasn't going to be very nice.

His hunches weren't usually far off the mark.

Chapter 3

Sabrina stood on the tarmac, her dark tresses blown by the wind. Two days ago she wouldn't have believed it if anyone had told her she'd be here at the tiny Lantana airport, waiting to be picked up and flown somewhere by somebody she didn't know. But she'd been told some amazing things over the phone, and the man she'd been speaking to, who called himself Dr. Morrow, had known what he was talking about. He'd spoken about a breakthrough in recombining the animal genes that she just had to see for herself. The only way Morrow would let her see, though, was as an employee for Visigen, which was his company.

She'd never heard of it, but Morrow explained that they kept a low profile because of work they were doing for the government. Maybe it was all bull, but she had to know the truth. It wouldn't do any harm to look into it, and Morrow had offered a very decent salary, one that made Nutech's offer seem paltry by comparison.

A low rumble presaged an afternoon thunderstorm. Well, it was 2:15 and her contact ought to be here any minute. If he was on time, she probably wouldn't get wet.

As she waited, the doubts began to bloom like poisonous flowers. They always did about something like this, but every time she'd backed out of something important, she'd regretted it later.

"Something like this," she whispered. "Who ever heard of something as secret as this?"

The meeting was highly unorthodox, but how else was she going to find out if Morrow's claims were for real?

Only twenty or thirty yards from where she stood, a helicopter began to descend onto the landing pad next to an airstrip. The machine's rotors pushed warm air at her and a moment later it was resting on the ground. The cockpit was a dark glass bubble polarized so that nobody could see who was inside. The word "Visigen" was enclosed in a clever oblong logo on the helicopter's fuselage.

A hatch opened and a man stepped out. He wore a laboratory smock and sunglasses, and his hair and beard were white. He walked toward her, smiled, and extended a hand.

"Dr. Fontaine," he said in a pleasant voice.

Sabrina shook his hand. "I'm delighted to meet you, Dr. Morrow."

His handshake was firm, yet gentle. He still clutched her fingers as he said, "I see that you've decided to take us up on our offer."

"I didn't have much choice," Sabrina replied. "In spite of all the intrigue, it's an offer I can't refuse."

Morrow smiled again. "I see that you have your bag with you. That's good. Our compound isn't terribly far, but you will probably want to stay overnight so that you can see everything."

"It will take two days to look the place over?"

"Yes, I think that's a fair estimate."

Another man emerged from the helicopter. He was younger than Dr. Morrow and also wore sunglasses. He picked up her suitcase and carried it back toward the landing pad.

"Well, then," Dr. Morrow said, "shall we begin your orientation by climbing aboard?"

Sabrina smiled. She was somewhat reassured by Dr. Morrow's courteous air. There was an almost hypnotic quality to his speech pattern that soothed her fears. He put his fingers on her shoulder and helped her step up into the chopper.

Inside, there was seating for four, quite a lot of room for a helicopter. There was even a luggage rack behind the black vinyl upholstery. The man who had put her suitcase in the rack sat next to the pilot, and Dr. Morrow took his place in the seat next to her. He continued to make small talk as the pilot spoke to the tower and they slowly lifted off the ground.

The thunderclouds were nearer now, and they headed right for them. Lightning played among the roiling gray woollike shapes as they passed over the storm and the copter banked, heading due west. That surprised Sabrina; she expected the labs to be either south in Fort Lauderdale or Miami, or north in Orlando.

Dr. Morrow smiled at her as if he could read her mind. "Yes, our compound is a bit off the beaten path. This way, we don't have so many people around asking us questions we aren't authorized to answer."

"I see."

The storm was soon behind them, and the blazing afternoon sunlight returned, though it was dimmed by the polarized glass of the cockpit. They flew over rectangular pastures and the crisscrossing blue lines that Sabrina recognized as canals. At first the flat land extended to the horizon, but then the tops of trees began to appear. The growth became thicker until it was transformed into a jungle. Sabrina knew that the ground here was marshy, swamplike. They were approaching the Everglades.

"Is your compound on the west coast of Florida?" she asked.

"No."

"You mean it's in the Everglades?"

Dr. Morrow smiled charmingly at her. "We maintain our privacy this way. There are many prying eyes who would like to see what we're doing."

They flew a little farther into the dark heart of the swamp. The chopper began to descend. All Sabrina could see were trees as they went straight down. In a moment they would collide with the uppermost boughs.

"Don't worry," Dr. Morrow said. "We'll be all right."

Sabrina glanced at him. He was smiling again. He seemed to be amused by the panic in her eyes. "Nothing to worry about," he said.

"Are you sure?" Sabrina closed her eyes as the treetops rose up to meet them.

She expected to hear the rending of wood and metal, feel the engine sputter, perhaps even explode as they plummeted to the ground. But nothing happened.

Sabrina slowly opened her eyes. They were passing through the trees as if they were ghosts. Below, long, gleaming buildings were laid out in an octagon. In the middle was something that looked like a Roman amphitheater, only oddly stylized. The architecture was like nothing she'd ever seen before.

At the compound's eight corners were towers on which were mounted projectors. They had passed through a hologram of a forest. No one would ever spot this place from the air in a million years. Sabrina had to admit it was very clever.

At that moment she noticed the guards' uniforms. Crimson. She'd seen them before on television and in the streets of Miami. At first they'd been welcome, but then their presence had turned into a nightmare. Visitors. But how could it be? They were all gone—the Red Dust toxin had seen to that.

She looked at Dr. Morrow, and he returned her gaze with paternal sincerity.

"We thought about trying to deceive you," he said, "but we decided that you would have found us out eventually."

Was she having a nightmare? She glanced around her in terror as the helicopter landed. She saw three white ships—skyfighters—around the pad, arranged in a triangle. Green, reptilian faces peered at them through dark glasses. She was trapped.

Her fear boiled over into anger. "You lied to me."

"Not really," Dr. Morrow replied. "Every scientific advance I mentioned exists here at the compound. I'm sure you'll find your stay very interesting—if you'll just adopt the correct attitude."

"Then you're taking me prisoner."

"Let's just say," Morrow told her as he opened the hatch, "that we're going to need your help." He gestured for her to climb out of the chopper.

Sabrina stared out at the steamy swamp dotted with the shining, alien buildings and spacecraft, all peopled by the uniformed reptilian invaders. She wanted to scream, but she remained silent.

Dr. Morrow reached out to help her down, but she shook off his hands and climbed down by herself.

Chapter 4

The dark side of Earth's single moon loomed on the screen before Medea. A dead world, with only the merest traces of water under its surface. Perhaps it would have once served her purposes, but that was millions of years ago. Some of the moons of the large gas giants in this solar system had water, but there was no industry in place to help her people suck it up and store it, as there was on Earth.

Even if there had been, she wouldn't have been interested now. The Terrans had angered her, and she intended to make them pay for their insolence. Her scientists were working on an antidote to the horrible red toxin at this very moment, and it wouldn't be long before they could take the fleet back to that blue and white planet and teach the monkeys who lived there a lesson. In the meantime, she would just have to wait.

A flicker of light on the console distracted her from her reverie.

She sat down to see what it was about, flicking a switch to receive the message. An officer appeared on the screen without his human makeup. It was good to see his natural scales and his tongue flicking pleasantly as he spoke.

"What is it?" Medea asked.

"Sir, we've received another message from the scientists stranded on Earth."

She nodded. "And they still want to know if we're going to attempt a rescue mission. Is that it?"

"Yes."

"All right. This time you can give them a definite answer."

"Can I tell them you'll send a ship?"

"No, I think we'll leave them right where they are for a while."

The officer looked shocked, yellow eyes darkening in confusion. "I don't understand, sir."

"You don't need to." Medea slammed her palm down on the switch and cut him off. She sat at the console, thinking for a few seconds, and then realized that everyone in the ship's command center was watching her.

She spun around in her chair. "Attend to your duties!" she snapped.

She got up and walked to the hatch. It hissed open, and she moved briskly through the ship's corridors until she came to her quarters. The command center was all very well for routine communications, but she wanted to talk to Morrow in private.

A moment later she was removing her makeup and placing her artificial eyes in their tray. She carefully peeled off the human face and removed the skin on her hands as if it were a pair of gloves. Then she sat down at her own console and contacted Morrow.

His face appeared on the screen. "Medea," he said.

"Dr. Morrow."

"It's very good of you to contact me personally. I hope you have good news for us."

"The concept of good is relative," Medea said.

Even though he wore his human makeup, Morrow's disappointment was obvious from his expression. "Then we must stay here?"

"I'm afraid so."

"Very well, then. If you think it's for the best."

"From what I have heard, Dr. Morrow, you have been

achieving positive results. I think it would be a shame to curtail your experiments now."

"I understand." Dr. Morrow nodded. "There are some developments you haven't heard of yet."

"Oh?" Medea flicked her forked tongue to show her interest.

"Yes, we have the assistance of human scientists."

"Excellent. You managed that even after our fleet was forced to leave Earth. That is remarkable. How did you enlist their aid?"

"Shall we say that they are not in a position to turn us down?" He smiled. A most convincing human expression, Medea thought. The technicians who had devised these disguises were to be congratulated.

"It seems that you're doing quite well, then. The Terrans have no idea that you're even on the planet. If you can maintain that kind of secrecy until you have shown the desired results, then you will have greatly helped the war effort and you will be rewarded."

Dr. Morrow bowed gratefully.

"I will be in communication with you on a regular basis from now on." With a flick of a talonlike finger, she shut off the transmission.

With Morrow and his minions working for her back on Earth, it wouldn't be long before she would be ready to attack the humans once again. They had been beaten the first time by a resistance force—and some very bad luck. Now Diana was imprisoned, but Medea had a resistance of her own working on Earth.

Her enemies would be very surprised when they saw the results. Very surprised, indeed. If Morrow's research turned out as she expected, she would crush Donovan and the resistance once and for all.

She rose and stretched her leathery limbs. Discipline on the ship was getting too lax, she thought. After she had rested, she would see to it that everyone wore their human disguises while on duty.

They would wear them until Earth was under her power.

Chapter 5

The road out to the reservation was nothing more than a raised gravel hump snaking through the swamp. T. J. Devereaux had never liked driving out here, and the Indians usually took care of their own business, but there was no way he could ignore a possible murder.

He drove deeper into the shade of the big banyans, wet ferns occasionally slapping the windshield. In a few minutes he caught sight of a shack he remembered belonging to an old swamp rat named Walter Miles. The Seminole village wasn't much farther away.

Soon he was pulling up to the cinder block recreation building and visitors' center. There were a few young men lounging on the steps. To the right and left were the shacks the Indians were forced to live in. Seminoles—Miccosuccee, really—still didn't have it so good, even in this enlightened age. Enlightened? Hell, there were still a lot of people around who believed the Visitors were our friends, and the resistance were a bunch of evil terrorists.

T.J. pulled up in the building's shade and got out of the jeep.

"Chief around?" he asked one of the four young fellows sitting on the steps.

The kid, sporting some kind of punk haircut and colorful Seminole clothing, didn't even look at him. T.J. had run into this sort of thing before on the reservation, so he didn't bother to ask again. They would just ignore him, the evil white-eyes. Shit.

It was sticky and hot inside. The paint on the corridor walls was peeling. T.J. suspected the school was in no better shape. It seemed as if things just kept getting worse for the Indians.

He knocked on the door at the end of the corridor.

"Come on in," said a soft voice.

T.J. opened the door. An old man with white hair and deep wrinkles in his brown face sat at a desk, reams of paper virtually covering its chipped Formica top.

"Well, what can I do for you, Sheriff?" Chief Martin Wooster asked. He leaned back and put his spidery hands on the taped-up armrests.

"Chief, I hear you've got a missing boy." T.J. took off his hat and fingered the damp sweatband inside.

"Got a lot of missing boys. How come this one interests you?"

"I got a call. Seems like his girl friend suspects foul play."

"Only been gone a day." The swivel chair groaned as the chief shifted his weight. "Might have just gone to Fort Lauderdale."

"That's not what the girl thinks."

"Oh? What do you think, Sheriff?"

Why was the old buzzard so damned hostile? T.J. had never done anything to him. "I don't want to make any assumptions, just find out if anything's happened to this kid."

"Well, maybe he just got himself drunk and went off someplace to sober up. Or maybe he's got himself a new squaw." The chief grinned at him mockingly.

"I didn't say that."

"But you're thinking it. You're thinking it's a pain in the ass you had to drive all the way out here just because some Indian girl is missing her boyfriend."

"Look, as far as I'm concerned the Seminoles have the same rights as anybody else."

"We're Miccosuccee."

"I know that. Seminole is a Creek word meaning 'runaway,' kind of a generic term."

Wooster looked surprised. His expression softened, and he said, "Look, Sheriff, we don't like it when outsiders come in. We're a pretty obscure group out here, and that's the way we want to keep it."

"I don't want to cause you any trouble, Chief. And I don't intend to bring a bus load of tourists with me next time I come out. As if there were any tourists in Kelleher County to bring."

Wooster almost smiled. "Okay, you've made your point. But how do we know you won't try to throw your weight around while you're out here."

"You don't," T.J. said. "So you'll just have to take my word for it—whatever that's worth to you."

"Never let it be said that Martin Wooster stood in the way of the law. I suppose you'll want to be talking to Marie Whitley?"

"Good place to start."

The chief got up and pointed out the window. "See that house, fourth one down, by those palmettos? That's Marie's mother's house."

T.J. nodded. "Thanks."

The chief sat back down and resumed his paperwork as if there had been no interruption.

Outside, T.J. found the four young men talking to a ruggedly built man in his late twenties, wearing a cane cowboy hat and a blue work shirt and jeans.

"I hear you're looking for Billy Tiger," he said.

"That's right."

"Why?" There was a defiant air about this young man that was more unsettling than the chief's almost polite needling. "I don't really owe you an explanation, now, do I?"

"You might."

"Why is that?"

"He's my brother."

T.J. nodded. "I'm T. J. Devereaux," he said, sticking out his hand.

Billy Tiger's brother looked at his hand as though it were a diamondback, but then he shook it firmly after a moment. "John Tiger."

"John, I got a call from a young woman who said your brother has been missing for well over twenty-four hours."

"So?"

"She said he was supposed to meet her yesterday afternoon, but she hasn't heard a word from him since night before last. She's worried."

"Sheriff, haven't you ever heard of men and women breaking up?"

"You think that's all there is to it?"

"Maybe."

"And maybe not. Look, John, I know you don't like outside interference in your affairs, but this could be serious."

"Billy will be back."

"I hope you're right. But I think I better talk to the girl."

"Do what you want, but you're wasting your time."

"We'll see."

T.J. turned and walked away from John Tiger and the others. God, it was hot. He could sure use a drink. Maybe the girl would offer him one. The way things were going, though, he doubted it.

There was a little metal nameplate on the Whitley place. It was tiny, but neater than most of the pathetic hovels. There was a little flower garden in front, with chrysanthemums, hibiscus, and bougainvillea in bloom. T.J. knocked on the front door.

A middle-aged woman came to the door. She looked at him angrily. "What do you want?" she demanded.

"I got a call from Ms. Whitley, ma'am. Is she your daughter?"

"Marie," the woman called, "somebody here for you." Without asking him inside, the woman backed away from the ragged screen door and vanished in the cool, dark recesses of the little house.

A moment later a girl came out. She was young and pretty,

with a very pleasant voice and a slender figure. T.J. tended to discount the theory about Billy Tiger running off just to get rid of her.

"Thank you for coming, Sheriff," she said.

"You're welcome, miss. Just doing my job."

"Please, come inside."

There was a television, an old vinyl sofa, and two chairs in the little living room. Marie got him a Coke from an ancient Kelvinator and sat down in the chair opposite him.

"Nobody wants to talk to me," T.J. said. "This isn't gonna be easy."

"They're afraid—and angry. There's something going on out in the swamp."

"What do you mean?" The ice-cold aluminum can felt good in his hand.

"A lot of people have disappeared, Sheriff, Not just Billy."

"Are you sure?"

"Positive. My people think it's the government."

"The government? Why would the government kidnap people?"

"I don't know. But there's a rumor going around that there's a big compound out in the Everglades. It could only be a government project, from the size and look of it."

"Interesting. Now, when exactly—as close to the minute as you can come—did you last see Billy Tiger?"

When he had finished questioning the girl, T.J. braved the angry looks of the young men once again and drove back toward Larkin, the Kelleher County seat. On the way, he stopped to talk to old Walter Miles.

By this time the sun was going down, and the swamp sounds were growing louder and louder. T.J. pounded on the shack's door for a minute. Place was too small for Walter not to hear him, even if he was dead drunk, so, when nobody answered, he tried the door. It was ajar.

The place was a mess. Chairs and a single table were overturned; cans, tin plates, pots, and pans were scattered on the log floor, and a box-spring mattress lay on its side against the stove.

Outside the crickets chirped; otherwise, it was still. The breezeless evening seemed to bear the overpowering odor of fear.

T.J. shook his head, thinking about how dubious he'd been while listening to Marie Whitley.

Now it looked as if he might have been mistaken.

Chapter 6

Jack slammed the phone down on its cradle. This was the fourth time he'd dialed Sabrina's number in the past hour. She should have been back by now; two days had gone by since the Nutech opening ceremony. Where the hell could she be? He'd taken a hotel room in town at a fancy new place that had plastic cards instead of room keys.

He sat on the edge of the bed, frustrated and angry and a bit afraid. The notion that something was wrong had gnawed away at him for over forty-eight hours. He had called Coach Shula and requested a day or two's leave. He had to get back to Miami soon or face a penalty when he finally did go back.

What difference did it make? He had to contact Sabrina before he left Boca Blanca. If she didn't answer the phone in the next few hours, he was going to call the police. He had asked himself several times if he was that worried, and in the end he decided that he was. He'd never felt this way about a woman before. He was furious, but he had no choice but to stay in "Silicon Beach," as Boca Blanca was known, at least until this thing was cleared up.

He threw himself onto the floor and started doing push-ups.

By the time he got to fifty, he knew he was going to call again as soon as he got off the floor. He did ten more and stood up, catching his breath for a minute before punching the numbers on the phone.

He let it ring six times and was just about to hang up when someone picked up on the other end.

"Sabrina!" Jack cried. "Where have you been? I've really been worried about you."

His heart was thumping wildly in his chest as he anticipated hearing her voice. But he went cold as a man's voice said: "Sorry to disappoint you, pal, but this is Sabrina's grandmother."

Jack held the phone away from his ear and looked at it as though it were a cobra about to strike. "Who the hell is this?" he demanded.

"I haven't got the time," the intruder said. He hung up.

Jack shook with rage. His face felt hot, and he was afraid he might crush the phone with his bare hands. There was a goddamn intruder in Sabrina's apartment, maybe burgling her possessions. Or perhaps it was someone who was involved in her disappearance. Well, he knew how to deal with him, whoever he was. Jack grabbed his keys and the hotel pass card. He was out the door in ten seconds, running down the stairwell in fifteen, and was in the parking lot in a minute flat.

He roared out of the parking lot as if it were the Indianapolis Speedway, heading for Interstate 95. This time of night there wasn't much traffic. He could get there in five or ten minutes.

"Make that four," he said, swerving around a car whose driver was only going a few miles over the speed limit. His tires screeched as he ran a red light and zoomed up the winding ramp to the highway.

He was at Sabrina's house in three and a half minutes, leaping out of the ZX without bothering to open the door. Every light in the house was on. Sabrina's car was in the carport.

Jack didn't bother to knock. If the door was locked, he would break it down. But there was no need for force; the knob turned easily in his big hand.

Jack had only been in Sabrina's house once before. She had moved in just two weeks ago. It was a single-story dwelling with a tiled roof, typical of the subtropical suburbs of South Florida. He was pretty sure he knew the layout. This was the living room he was standing in. The kitchen adjoined it, and there was a dining room on the other side of the wall, opening into the living room. Ring-around-a-rosy. If the intruder had a gun, Jack could dive into the kitchen. And then he would have his choice of which door to go for. It was better than no chance at all. If the guy had no gun—well, Jack might feel sorry for him later, might even send him a fruit basket in the hospital.

Spreading his feet wide apart, Jack lowered his shoulders while keeping his head up. He almost took a three-point stance, but then he remembered that this was no game.

Silent as a cat, he sprang into the kitchen.

Nobody there.

Jack pressed himself against the kitchen cabinets, trying to make as small a target as possible. The air conditioner was on, but he was sweating badly in spite of it.

Moving so low to the floor that his chest almost brushed the rug, Jack went into the dining room. It too was empty.

The china cabinet was open, as if someone had been looking inside it and forgotten to close it when he heard the front door open.

Maybe the intruder was gone, scared off.

And then again, maybe not. Jack would just have to find out the hard way.

There were three rooms left: the master bedroom, the guest room, and the den. The den was closest. Swiftly and silently, Jack entered it.

The den was a mess. Drawers hung out of the desk, papers were scatterd all over the floor, and the swivel chair was overturned. Somebody was looking for something—and he wanted it very badly.

Jack edged along the wall, out into the hallway. He glanced into the guest room, the only room without a light on. It was untouched, as far as he could see in the long shard of light thrown by a dining room lamp.

His heart pounding, Jack inched toward Sabrina's bedroom. If the intruder was still in the house, he had to be in here. There just wasn't anyplace else to look.

Jack wanted to be invisible, to still his breathing and his heartbeat so that the intruder would never see him, hear him, or even smell him. He could still turn away, go back out into the warm Florida night, and get in his car. He could go back to the hotel and call the police.

He could do a lot of things, but he wasn't built that way. Jack jumped into the room.

A man stood there in Sabrina's ransacked bedroom. He stood about six feet and was thirty-five to forty years old. He wore a leather jacket. His hair was thin, and he was broad shouldered. His face had a nasty expression, as if the guy was pleased he'd been caught.

"Hello, sailor," the intruder said.

Jack was just about to tear him apart when he felt something cold touch his head behind the right ear. He knew what it was, even though he couldn't see it.

"Smile," said a voice from behind him.

Jack grimaced.

"Now, you're probably wondering what we're doing here," the man in the leather jacket said.

"I know what you're doing here, scumbag," Jack said through gritted teeth.

"Do you? What are we doing here, then?"

"You're robbing my fiancée's apartment."

"Use your head, jocko," the man snapped. "Do you see any missing stereos, silverware, jewelry? Anything like that?"

It was true. "Then, why are you tearing the place apart?"

"Looking for clues, big boy. Just like in a mystery."

"Clues?" Jack said, his spirits sinking. "Clues to what?"

"To where your girlfriend has been taken by the Visitors."

Chapter 7

Jack mulled over what he'd been told. "How do I know you're being straight with me?" he asked. "I mean, with this guy holding a gun to my head."

"Put it down, Chris. Just to show the man we can be reasonable."

The icy metal was gone, and Jack heard the click of the pistol's safety. Knowing that he'd never have another chance like this, he swung around, lowering his body at the same time. He threw a cross-body block on the gunman, sending him smashing into a table. A lamp, makeup, and a box of Kleenex scattered, and Sabrina's big oval mirror shattered into a thousand pieces.

The guy was big, and he went down hard. He still had some fight in him, but three quick punches put him on the floor for the rest of the fight.

Jack turned his attention to the man in the leather jacket.

"Wait a minute, friend," the man was saying, his wise-ass expression gone now. He waved one hand expressively while he talked. "We're trying to help you. Let's not be hasty."

Jack didn't listen to him, and he didn't watch the gesturing hand. He saw the other hand go inside the jacket, and that was all he needed.

He was on the guy in an instant. The first right hook probably would have done the job, but Jack gave him four more as he started to sag toward the floor.

The guy landed on the overturned mattress, bounced once, and was still.

Breathing heavily from his exertions, Jack took their guns. He went into the kitchen and removed the ice-making tray from the refrigerator. He went back into the bedroom and dropped ice cubes on them until they began to stir.

"All ready to visit the city jail?" he asked as the gunman rubbed his jaw. He turned and poked the other one with his shoe. "How about you, joker?"

"They won't hold us in jail," Leather Jacket said, sitting up on the floor.

"Want to bet?" But in spite of the advantage he had gained, Jack knew this was no ordinary burglary. He waited for them to explain themselves before going to the phone. After all, he had the guns now. There was no need to hurry. "Tell me why they won't hold you."

"We're CIA. My name is Ham Tyler. This is my partner, Chris."

"Ham Tyler. Where have I heard that name before? And what was that bit about Visitors taking Sabrina?"

"You heard it right," Ham Tyler said, delicately fingering a bruise on his cheek.

"The Visitors are gone, Tyler."

"Not all of them."

"Come on. They were driven off the planet by the Red Dust. They come back and they die."

"Listen, my hard-hitting friend. Has it ever occurred to you that a technology eight hundred years ahead of our own might be able to come up with an antidote?"

Jack said nothing. He had thought of it, and there had been a lot of talk about that possibility in the weeks following the Visitors' departure. Now there was little speculation on the subject. It was almost as if there had never been an invasion at all. The complacency that had so quickly set in was a little bit frightening, now that he thought about it.

"I can see that you have considered it." Tyler got slowly and shakily to his feet. "I'm here to tell you that those lizards have done more than just consider it. They've done it."

"Ham Tyler." Now Jack remembered where he'd seen this guy. "You were with Donovan and Julie Parrish, weren't you? I saw you on television."

"Yeah, not a good thing for a CIA man to be seen on the six o'clock news. Makes covert operations a little more difficult. Thanks for changing my face a little."

Ham helped Chris up. "Who do you work for, man?" Chris asked, his three hundred pounds nearly putting Ham back on the floor.

"Don't you recognize him?" Ham said. "He's a flanker for the Dolphins—Jack Stern."

"No kidding?"

"No kidding," Jack said.

"Well, since you're a football fan, Ham, maybe I won't turn you in."

"Thanks. We'll mention it to your girl friend when we find her."

"You have some idea where she might be?" Jack asked.

"Maybe."

Jack didn't have to think it over. He had no other lead as to Sabrina's whereabouts. "I'm going with you."

"Huh?" Chris still looked a little groggy. "No, man. Me and Ham work better on our own."

"I said I'm going with you." Jack hefted the .45 automatic in one hand and the Walther in the other. "You aren't in any position to argue at the moment."

"Man's got a point," Ham said, picking up a shard of glass with which to examine the damage Jack had done to his face.

"That doesn't cut any ice with me," Chris said.

"Take it easy," Ham told him, dropping the glass sliver on the floor. "Mr. Stern might come in handy."

Chris appraised Jack with one raised eyebrow. "You think so?"

"I think so," Ham said.

It was easy to see who the boss was.

"Don't worry about this mess," Ham said. "We'll clean it up after we get back."

The three of them started toward the front door. As they passed the china closet, Jack asked, "Why did you look in there?"

"Why not?" Ham said. "It seemed as good a place as any to start."

They went out under the stars, ready to begin their search.

Chapter 8

Blue light spun around and around Billy, and he felt a terrible throbbing, as if his head were swelling to twice its normal size. Was he having a nightmare?

Crackling, sizzling noises filled the air around him. And there was a smell that reminded him of thunderstorms. And those yellow eyes were watching him . . . watching him . . . watching him. . . .

And it hurt. God, how it hurt. Why were they doing this to him? He'd never harmed them.

He'd never harmed anyone but himself. And still the terrible blue light spun around him endlessly. How long had it been, now? Where was he?

At the bottom of a swamp.

They were watching him through their cold, reptilian eyes. The 'gators. The ripple on the water's surface was above him now, not next to his canoe.

He was in the 'gators' world now.

How could he breathe here? How could they keep him alive underwater? And why?

They said 'gators liked to let their meat rot before they ate it.

30

Maybe that's what they were doing to him—waiting for him to rot before they ate him.

No! He was still alive. As long as he was alive, they couldn't have him. He would fight the 'gators. He wouldn't let himself down as he had done before, back among those reptiles at the university.

He had felt their cold stare. They came from a different world than his—a world of privilege, a world full of people who always got their way. Reptiles. Billy felt as though they would eat him up, always so polite, always knowing just what to say and when to say it, always acting so understanding toward the Indian boy, the affirmative-action, token Seminole in the classroom, like a goldfish in a bowl.

He had never been so alone in the Everglades, even while drifting miles from the reservation among the herons and the cranes. Never so alone. . . .

"I am your friend," a strange, grating voice said from somewhere beyond the flickering blue beam that danced around him here in his fish tank.

"Did you hear me? I said I am your friend."

"I heard you."

"Do you believe I am your friend?"

"No."

A searing pain shot through Billy, beginning at his toes and traveling all the way to his head. He thought his skull would explode. His body shook as if ten thousand volts were passing through him.

"Once you clearly understand that I am your friend, then the pain will stop," the voice said.

"No," Billy moaned.

"Those who have hurt you in the past are responsible for the pain you suffer now," the voice went on. "These are not your people. You owe them nothing. Look how much they hurt you, Billy."

A jolt of pain shook him; it was much worse than anything he had ever felt in his entire life. They were trying to kill him, but who were they? Was it the 'gators? Or was it something else?

V

"You think of them as your own people," the voice said, "while they put you through this. You fool. I want to help you."

"No. *You* are hurting me, not them."

"Not me, Billy. Them."

A monstrous surge of pain coursed through Billy. He would have fallen to the floor, but something held him up. Something he couldn't see.

His father, Paul, held him by one hand. His mother held him by the other. He looked up at them, and they smiled, white teeth showing in their brown faces.

Ahead of them, Johnny walked, calling for them to catch up with him. Billy would be just like him when he got bigger, he hoped.

His dad let go of his hand. His father was wearing a uniform. He had to go back. To Vietnam.

To die.

And his mother cried. She cried every day and every night for a long time. And then she got sick. They said it was cancer.

And she went away too. To a hospital. She got weaker and weaker, and then she died, just like Paul.

And John and Billy were alone.

Alone.

"You will not be alone anymore," the voice said. "For I am your friend."

Maybe it was true. He was alone now. He no longer had Johnny. He had been taken away from Johnny—and from Marie.

Another cycle of terrible pain shook him to his very soul. But still he hung on to the train of thought that the pain was intended to wipe out. Marie.

She loved him, and he had been taken from her—and from John.

And the one who said he was his friend was the one who had taken him from his loved ones and brought him here to torment him.

"Liar!" Billy screamed. "You're not my friend! You're my enemy!"

Cycle after cycle of increasing pain followed. Billy knew they were going to kill him, but he didn't care. He would not allow them to take his mind.

The waves of pain were so intense now that he could see nothing, hear nothing, feel nothing but the agony that stiffened and vibrated his body.

And then the cycles began to decline somewhat. At first he thought he was dying, but the pain shrank down to nothing but exhaustion, and the blue beam spun around him slower and slower until there was no light at all.

Billy fell backward. He hit his head, but it didn't hurt. He was still in the aqueous, transparent chamber, but it had become dark and silent.

He heard footsteps somewhere; they were coming toward him. He tried to open his eyes, but he could only manage it for a second or two.

There were lizard men all around him. They were all dressed in red uniforms except for one, who was all in white.

"This one is strong," the lizard in white said, flicking his forked tongue. "He may be just the one we've been searching for. Take him to the laboratory."

Billy felt claws on his limbs; they picked him up and carried him out of the fish tank. The 'gators still had him, but they had not yet broken him.

He wondered groggily what they would do with him next. Could they have something even worse in store for him? He was spared thinking about the possibilities as he slipped into unconsciousness.

Chapter 9

"We don't want an air boat," Ham said. "Too noisy and too conspicuous. We want something quiet, like a canoe. Good enough for the Seminoles, good enough for us."

"What if we have to get out fast?" Chris asked.

"Then we scatter and hide in the swamp. They'd be able to track an air boat easily, but three men on foot will be a lot more difficult."

"Look," Jack said as he poured himself a cup of coffee, "how do we know they've taken Sabrina into the Everglades?"

"We don't. Not for sure. But we do know a woman was picked up by a chopper on Friday at Lantana airport. The tower report says they headed due west out into the 'glades."

Jack nodded. It was by far the most substantial lead they had had up to now. He could have knocked himself out from now till doomsday and never come up with anything else. He'd always wondered if what they said about the CIA was true. Apparently it was. It was going to be interesting working with these two guys. Despite what had happened last night, Jack was beginning to gain some respect for them.

"Stern, you're absolutely certain you want to go along on this mission?" Ham Tyler said.

"Of course I do. I'm going to marry Sabrina. Do you think I'm just going to let a bunch of lizards have her without putting up a fight?"

"Whoa, Lone Ranger." Ham put up his hand. "It's one thing to be gung ho on the football field. But these lizards aren't playing a game. They shoot to kill. And if they don't kill you, what they do with you after they catch you could be worse than dying."

"A fate worse than death, huh?" Jack said. "You think Sabrina is going to be raped by a lizard?"

"Stranger things have happened," Ham said. "Let's hope they just want her scientific knowledge."

Jack was surprised to hear something that sounded like concern coming out of the mouth of the usually cynical Ham. He had known a lot of tough guys, both on the playing field and in the service; they often weren't so bad once they got used to you. Ham struck him as a man who had started out with a desire to help his country, who had somehow become so involved in the intricacies of his career that he had almost lost sight of human values. His career frequently involved killing people, after all, and that would make the best of men, and women, a little grim.

"Okay, let's get some rest. Wake-up call at six," Chris said.

"Can't we get started now?" Jack asked.

"Don't be a wise guy," Chris said, mimicking Curly of the Three Stooges so perfectly that Jack couldn't help laughing. Ham laughed too, and so did Chris. They laughed at the way they were laughing, and then they laughed at that. Jack laughed so hard his eyes watered, and it felt good. He lay down on the hotel bed, realizing that he hadn't cracked a smile for days before this.

"All right," Ham said, following Chris's bulk through the door, "we'll see you in the morning, Stern. Don't get lost."

"Right."

A moment later they were gone. Jack lay on the bed, restive, eager to go after the lizards who had taken Sabrina. He knew

he should get some sleep, and he turned out the lights and shut
his eyes.

"Big game tomorrow, Jack" he said aloud. "You need your
rest."

But he couldn't doze off, thinking of what might be
happening to Sabrina. Hard as it might be to accept, he'd rather
learn that she'd run off with some other guy than this. Well,
Ham could be wrong. The CIA had been wrong before.

But this time Jack had the bad feeling that there was no
mistake.

Chapter 10

Billy didn't know exactly how long he'd been in the red chamber. At first, he hadn't minded. They fed him here, gave him water, and inflicted very little pain.

Every once in a while he was strapped down to a table, and one of the 'gator men took a little knife and scraped some skin off his arm or back.

That was all they did to him here, not like in the transparent chamber with the blue beam spinning around him.

"Why are you doing this?" he'd sometimes ask them when they were scraping his skin, "Are you trying to find out what makes humans tick?"

They never answered. They just scraped away silently in the dim red light as if he were a plant specimen.

Well, maybe to these 'gators he was like a plant. Maybe they were just trying to figure out what seasoning would go best on him before they cooked him and ate him. That would explain why they kept him here, feeding him. Fattening him up for the kill.

Somehow Billy didn't believe they were going to eat him, though. Not just yet. They had something else in mind. He was some kind of guinea pig, some kind of lab animal they were testing.

Not a white rat. He'd been allowed to run no mazes. Unless they were examining his mental mazes. But they couldn't find out what he was thinking by taking skin-tissue samples. No, whatever they were up to, it was biological, not psychological.

The door whooshed open, and a lizard in a white smock entered, carrying a food tray.

"How ya doing?" Billy said.

The alien set the tray down on a flat surface that Billy had been using for his dining table. At first he had been bothered by the trays being in lizard hands. The first time they had brought food, he didn't want to touch it. But he'd still been weak from the ordeal in the transparent chamber, so he had forced himself to eat a few bites.

The food was odd—lumpy pastes and starchy rings—but he was getting used to it. He had to keep up his strength or he'd be unable to make a break for freedom when the time came.

And the time would come. He had to believe that the time would come. Otherwise, he might as well lie down and die right now.

Billy had tried to scratch lines in the wall to amuse himself, but he couldn't damage the smooth material, even with the odd little spoon they had given him to eat with. They gave him nothing to write on, no books or magazines, no television; food and water only. Billy had never been so bored in his entire life, even at the University of Florida.

At least his boredom gave him time to plan his escape. Just how he would go about it was still rather vague in his mind. One of the times when they brought in food, he would jump the guard, perhaps. Or he could make a weapon of the spoon.

The spoon . . . He found himself using his left hand more and more whenever he ate. He knew from the lizards' occupation of Earth that it meant conversion was taking hold.

He fought it, forcing himself to use his right hand whenever he slipped into using his left. At times it took a great effort of will to switch hands, but he always managed it, even when it left him weak and trembling.

He picked up the spoon and poised it over the lukewarm green paste on the tray, consciously using his right hand. As he lowered the spoon, he began to shake. All he had to do to stop the shaking was put the spoon in the other hand, he knew, and the temptation was strong. But he wouldn't do it, even if it killed him.

Holding his right wrist with the fingers of his left hand, he plunged the glop into his mouth and swallowed. The second bite wasn't quite so difficult, and soon he was eating with almost normal ease.

Just as he was finishing his meal, the door slid open again. A man stood on the threshold—at least, he looked like a man. He was wearing a smock and had white hair and a beard.

"May I come in?" he asked.

His mouth full, Billy managed to get down the last of the green glop. "Why not?" he replied.

The man entered. "Mr. Tiger, I am Dr. Morrow, the director of this scientific compound." He extended a hand.

Billy declined to shake it. "Why are you holding me here?"

Dr. Morrow slowly withdrew his hand. "We just want to conduct a few tests."

"And when you're finished with your tests?"

"What happens to you then will depend upon your behavior while you are our guest."

"Guest! I'm a prisoner, a guinea pig for your experiments. How dare you call me a guest?"

"Very well. You are a prisoner, Mr. Tiger. Does my calling you that make you feel better."

"Yes, it does. You lizards don't seem to understand how important the truth is to a human being. If I pretended I was your guest and that you'd let me go if I cooperated, it would be a lie."

"How do you know it isn't true?"

"Common sense tells me it can't be. I know what you and your kind have done in the past."

"That was the past," Dr. Morrow said smugly.

"Oh, come on. Do you think I've forgotten that you tortured me in that conversion chamber until you almost fried my brain?

I know you're a little disappointed that it didn't work, but that's just the breaks, I guess."

"On the contrary. We are delighted that conversion didn't work with you, Mr. Tiger."

"What?" Billy was taken aback just as he was getting wound up. "What did you say?"

"I said that we are pleased that conversion didn't work in your case."

"Explain."

"Very well." Dr. Morrow paused, and then began to speak dramatically. "Because of your strength, your courage, your—intransigence, if you will, you have been chosen as the progenitor of a new race."

"A new race?"

"You will be its father, Mr. Tiger. And it will have the qualities that we admire so in you. Those qualities and more."

"More? What do you mean?"

"That will soon be evident, Mr. Tiger. Good day." Dr. Morrow stepped back through the door as it slid open to let him pass. A moment later he was gone.

Imprisoned in his cage again, Billy realized that he might have just missed his best opportunity to escape. He had been so confused by what Dr. Morrow had said that he never thought of jumping him when the door opened.

What could Morrow have meant? He, Billy Tiger, the father of a new race? Absurd.

But the nonsense Morrow spouted had made Billy miss the best chance to escape he might ever have.

Chapter 11

Jack got his wake-up call at six o'clock, just as he had been promised. At least they weren't going to slip away without him. That little confrontation in Sabrina's house must have convinced Tyler that he could use Jack when the rough stuff started.

After a shower and shave, Jack put on jeans and a work shirt, threw the rest of his things in a bag, and went down to check out of the hotel. He met Ham and Chris in the parking lot. They were riding in a four-wheel-drive Land-Rover with a rack on top carrying three canoes.

"High-tech, Stern," Ham said as Jack threw his gear into the Land-Rover. "We'll drive in as far as we can go, and then we'll paddle the rest of the way. This way, we'll catch 'em by surprise."

"I hope so," Jack said, worrying more and more about what had become of Sabrina. And, if the Visitors did have her, how they would get to her to bring her back.

"Let's saddle up, boys," Tyler said. Jack got in and they drove to Alligator Alley, a road heading due west out of Fort Lauderdale. They seldom spoke, and when they did it was usually to consult the map or express some other practical consideration. The sun rose steadily behind them as they cut across the swamps.

It was almost eleven before they turned off the highway onto a two-lane road that led them, within an hour, to a gravel road whose banks sloped into the murky water of the Everglades.

Chris was driving now. He had switched with Ham about ninety minutes earlier. As the tires crunched along, Jack became increasingly concerned. One bad decision and they'd be at the bottom of the swamp.

"Take it easy," Jack said at last. "We want to get there in one piece."'

Chris glowered at him.

"We don't have any time to waste," Ham said. "Keep driving, Chris."

It occurred to Jack that he was dealing with two lunatics. He had read about resistance fighters in Ireland who wanted to keep on fighting even after the truce. And there was Jesse James, who kept on fighting for the Confederacy long after Appomattox. Maybe Sabrina had run off with some other guy, or maybe she'd done just what she said in her note. Of course, if the latter were correct, she should be home by the time he returned from this little adventure with two CIA men. If he returned. They seemed determined to take unnecessary risks. Unnecessary unless they were right about the Visitors.

In any event, it was too late to back down now.

"Ho-lee!" Chris slammed on the brakes. The Land-Rover swerved, the tires kicking up gravel.

Jack shut his eyes, but not before he saw the police car careening right toward them. There was barely enough room for one car on this road, let alone two.

The Land-Rover spun around. Jack saw Chris's cigarettes fly across the dashboard and out the passenger side. He said his prayers as the front end swung out over the muddy water.

The tumult from the shouting, the roaring engine, and the crunching gravel ended even more abruptly than it had begun.

The three of them sat in breathless silence for a moment. A big man, wearing a broad-brimmed sheriff's hat and uniform, leaped out of the stalled patrol car and stalked over to the Land-Rover.

"Where the hell do you think you're going, boy?" the sheriff demanded. "There's a speed-limit sign posted back there, says twenty-five miles an hour."

"Right, Sheriff," Ham said. "But this is an emergency."

The sheriff rolled his eyes. But when Ham produced identification, he began to look a little more attentive.

"See-Eye-Ay—well, I'll be goddammed."

The tension level dropped a bit, and Jack noticed for the first time how sore his right shoulder and side were from being crushed against the vehicle door. Ham had been fortunate enough to be in the middle, where he was cushioned by Chris and Jack. Jack got out and walked on the gravel, swinging his arm and stretching. After a minute he decided he was all right.

"So what's the big emergency?" the sheriff asked. "Russians gonna parachute down into the 'glades or something?"

"Worse than that, Sheriff"—Ham studied the officer's name tag—"Devereaux."

"Some would have you believe you can't get no worse than that. What have you got? Cubans? Salvadorans?"

"Visitors."

The Sheriff had been looking off into the ominously dark growth blanketing the swamp. He did a double take. "Visitors? I thought they were all gone."

"That's what everybody thinks, Sheriff. And that's why they're doubly dangerous right now."

"Well, that's a very interesting theory, Mr. Tyler. I don't think I buy it, but you seem to. I don't guess you were speeding through here just for the fun of it, so I'm not gonna give you a ticket. Somebody in Washington would probably just rip it up for you anyway."

"Thanks, Sheriff." Ham started back toward the Land-Rover.

"Not so fast, Mr. Tyler. I got a proposition for you."

This time it was Ham who rolled his eyes. "And what might that be?"

"Well, there've been some funny things going on around here."

"What kind of funny things?"

"People just up and disappearing. Dropping out of sight just like they were possums caught in a snare."

Ham nodded knowingly. "That's our scaly friends at work, Sheriff."

"You'd bet on it?"

"Damn right."

"Seems to me there might be some other explanation, but I'd like to go along with you for a while. See what you turn up."

Ham and Chris looked at each other. Chris shrugged.

"Sure. I guess we can use a little extra help."

"Thanks," T. J. Devereaux said. "Now, let's see if we can get that rig of yours back on the road here, so we can get started."

Chapter 12

Her biological clock told Sabrina that it was almost time for her daily propaganda dose. She couldn't really be sure, since she had no way of telling what time it was or, for that matter, what day it was.

The door to her pristine chamber slid open and Dr. Thorkel entered. He was a pleasant, bald man in his late fifties, whom Sabrina had met once or twice in a professional capacity.

"How are you today, Dr. Fontaine?" he asked.

"As well as can be expected."

"Have you seen anyone being eaten yet?"

Sabrina said nothing. The last time Thorkel had visited her, they had talked about the Visitors eating people, something which she had thought everyone knew about by now. Thorkel was oblivious to the truth. He wanted to believe that the Visitors were here to help mankind, even after all that had happened.

"My dear Dr. Fontaine, I have seen things in this compound that are *so* wonderful. If we can obtain such knowledge from the Visitors, any minor misunderstandings between our two races must surely mean very little. For the good of mankind, we must cooperate with them, don't you see?"

"Dr. Thorkel," Sabrina replied, trying to remain polite, "you are being handed a bill of goods. You were here all during their attempt to seize control of our world, so it's understandable that you have been brainwashed into believing what they want you to believe."

"Brainwashed? Has it ever occurred to you that you might have been brainwashed by the terrorists who've tried to drive away the greatest hope mankind ever had?"

"I've never met a terrorist in my life. I worked in a lab where the senior scientists were taken away. They either came back spouting Friends of the Visitors slogans, or they didn't come back at all."

"Perhaps a few were detained."

"Detained? They were never seen again. They were lunch for a bunch of Visitors, most likely."

Thorkel shook his head sadly. "The Visitors only want you to see the truth. If you persist in believing this nonsense, they'll have to assist you in learning what the truth really is."

"Oh, Doctor," she said contemptuously, "you make me ill. You've rationalized being a traitor to your own people. If somebody has to lecture me on the wonders of the Visitors' technology, let it be Dr. Morrow. At least he's working for his own."

"He's working for us too, Dr. Fontaine. Don't you see?"

"No, I don't."

"Surely as a scientist you perceive knowledge as universal. We must put aside our petty squabbles and work together for the good of intelligent beings everywhere."

"Tell the Visitors to put down their weapons. Then we might be able to work together once they stop trying to exploit us and our resources."

"I thought better of you, Dr. Fontaine. I had no idea you could be so insular in your thinking."

Sabrina turned away. She had no further desire to speak to Dr. Thorkel, now or ever. She ignored him until he left her prison cell.

Just before the door whooshed shut, she heard something from outside her cell that chilled her. It was a horrible, wailing scream. It sounded half-human at best, a terrible, animal cry with the pathos only a man or woman could lend it. For the first time Sabrina wanted the door to shut, rather than hope that it remained open so that she might get away. At that moment she only wished to cut off that anguished scream.

Her relief when the door shut was almost physical. She fell back on the bed, quaking in fear. The sound she had just heard had affected her in a way she'd never felt before. An atavistic, almost animallike fear had gripped her.

She never wanted to hear such a thing again, but she knew she would. They were always watching her, and they must have seen her reaction.

Sooner or later, they would use it against her.

Billy Tiger had heard the cries too. Sometimes the monstrous sounds woke him up at night. No attempt was made to shield him from it.

A form of torture? Somehow Billy didn't think so. More likely the result of one of their experiments. But what sort of creature could make a cry like that? He rolled over on his stomach in bed, covering his head with a pillow. They could drive him mad with that sound.

There was something familiar about it. That was what disturbed him most. He'd heard that voice a thousand times, it seemed, but not with this horrid, distorted quality. Whose voice could it be?

He ticked off the people he'd known who had disappeared, and was certain it was none of them. He lay awake thinking about it for quite some time, and then at last he began to doze. In his dreams he was alone, just as he had been in the conversion chamber. The 'gators were after him again, but now he recognized them for what they were. They chased him through the corridors of the compound, baring their yellow, daggerlike teeth. He fought them, eluded them, surviving somehow in this place of horrors. He opened one door after another, searching for a way out.

At last he came to a door behind which was darkness. This, he was certain, was the way out. But there was someone—or something—in there, blocking his way.

He tried to fight it, but he couldn't. He saw it, and he screamed. He screamed again. And again.

He awoke to the sound of his own screaming. And it was that very sound that froze his heart. For he screamed with the voice of the half-human thing he had heard outside the door.

Chapter 13

Riding in the sheriff's car, Jack noticed a sign saying that there was a Seminole reservation five miles farther up the road.

"That's where Billy Tiger came from," T.J. said. "And that's where he ain't come home to."

Jack looked at the burly lawman. "You say his girl friend called you about his disappearance?"

"Yup. Worried as hell. The chief and his brother said he probably ran off with another woman, but she wouldn't swallow that."

"People usually know when they're being jilted. But when things are going okay and somebody vanishes, you've got to be a little worried."

T.J. took a packet of gum out of his shirt pocket. He offered a stick to Jack, who declined, and then removed one, shoved it into his mouth, and started chewing. "Them two CIA men are a pair beats three of a kind. Seems more like a married couple than partners."

"They're close, all right." Jack turned his head and glanced at the Land-Rover following T.J.'s patrol car. "When you suggested we split up, I was relieved. Those guys are so used to taking risks, they do crazy things even when they don't have to."

"Just a coupla fun-loving boys." T.J. chuckled. "Knew some like 'em when I was in the Army back in Korea."

"Well, even though I know they have their uses, I'm glad I'm not riding with them anymore."

"So long as we're in front of them, they can't drive too fast. Don't matter how fast they go now, though. We're just about there."

T.J. turned off the road, onto an even narrower one that seemed like a tunnel through the overgrown vegetation. The fronds and tree limbs were so low they often scraped the roof of the car. It was worse for Ham and Chris in the Land-Rover.

At a small embankment, actually just a mound protruding out of the brown water, T.J. stopped and shut off his engine. Jack got out of the patrol car and stretched, peering into the midday darkness of the Everglades.

"This is where Billy Tiger pushed his canoe into the water," T.J. said. "Nobody's seen him since."

The Land-Rover pulled up behind them, and Ham and Chris joined them a few seconds later. Both of them were silent.

"Now," T.J. said, "I might believe Billy ran off with a woman except for one thing. He's not the only one who's gone, and some of the other missing persons ain't exactly the most eligible bachelors around, unlike Billy. There was an old derelict named Walter Miles, who checked out about the same time Billy did. Trouble was, nobody was around to care about Walter. But he's gone, same as Billy."

"So you're beginning to lend my argument a little credence," Ham said. "I knew you were a sensible man, Sheriff Devereaux."

"Call me T.J. Everybody does."

"We brought three canoes."

"I noticed," T.J. said, slapping at a mosquito on his neck. "Jack and me can take one, and you boys can each have your own. We'll cover more ground if we all go in separate directions. Then rendezvous back here at six."

They unfastened the canoes and took them down. Chris went

fast, setting the sleek green craft in the water and climbing aboard without even getting the heels of his combat boots wet. His light brown hair streamed behind him as he paddled easily into the swamp. Ham was right behind him, and Jack carried the third canoe to the water and set it down. T.J. got in and told him to push.

Jack pushed, soaking himself to his knees before he managed to get into the canoe. T.J. didn't laugh, but Jack sensed that he was amused to see how clumsy the famous ball player was off the field. Oh well, Jack thought. To each his own sport.

After they drifted a few seconds, T.J. turned and asked politely, "Jack, don't you intend to paddle this thing?"

"Oh." He supposed he would have to, since there was only one paddle and he was sitting in the back. He plopped the oar into the water, creating a splash that got both of them wet.

"Cut it into the water sidewise, Jack," T.J. said calmly. "Then sort of turn your wrists. That way the paddle's got something to work against, but you won't give us a shower every time you stroke."

Jack chuckled. "You learn something new every day," he said, stroking the way T.J. told him. It worked pretty well, and Jack soon found himself getting into the spirit of it. It was good exercise for the arms and shoulders, and even for the legs and torso. The two men fell silent as they moved through the swamp. It was an ancient world, Jack thought; you wouldn't be surprised to see a dinosaur lift its scaly head out of the water and roar. The huge trees, with their twisted roots submerged, the fungus, the vines and creepers, and the silent rippling of the water where there was no current all added to the notion that this was a prehistoric world. He remembered his paleontology professor saying that alligators and crocodiles were on the earth before the dinosaurs, come to think of it. Those babies were built to survive.

"Listen," T.J. said with uncharacteristic sharpness. He held up his right hand in command. "Hear that?"

Jack was a little annoyed that his reverie had been disturbed, but then he heard it too. A low hum coming from behind a stand of cypress trees growing out of a muddy embankment.

And then he saw them: ten, maybe twelve of them. They glided through the air on silver disks, coming from between the trees.

Visitors!

Chapter 14

T.J. reached for his sidearm as the aliens started firing. The water all around them hissed as blue beams searched for Jack and T.J.

"You got a gun, Jack?" T.J. shouted, squeezing off a round. "No, I know you don't."

One of the aliens spewed green liquid out of its neck, somersaulting into the water with a huge splash. His disk wobbled and smacked into the embankment.

T.J. ducked, a beam burning a neat hole in the crown of his hat. Nevertheless, he hung on to his .38.

"You okay?" Jack shouted.

"Just my hat," T.J. replied, firing his pistol again after carefully taking aim. This time he missed, and the Visitor swerved right over him, hitting the edge of the boat with a beam.

The Visitor was still looking back over his shoulder when he passed over Jack. Hoping he wouldn't overturn the canoe, Jack leaped to his feet and swung the paddle like a baseball bat. He caught the Visitor square in the stomach. Hissing, he flew off his disk.

T.J. blew another one off with a well-aimed shot, but they were completely encircled now, at least eight Visitors swarming around them like buzzards over a dead animal.

One of the disks was wobbling aimlessly, its rider in the water. It veered toward them as if it might hit the canoe.

"Watch out!" T.J. shouted. He fired at it, but the shot failed to deflect the disk. It went over his head then began to ascend.

"Hold on!" Jack yelled. He jumped straight up out of the canoe and grabbed hold of the disk with both hands. He could feel it vibrating as he swung his legs back and forth. T.J. had a moment's respite from the Visitors' attack as they stopped to watch the amazing spectacle of Jack throwing one leg onto the antigravity platform and climbing atop it as it soared three yards over the swamp. He was squatting on it now, and he looked up to see that he was on a collision course with a cypress tree. "How do you steer this thing?" he screamed.

Before he could learn how, the tree was upon him. He just missed the trunk, and he was too low to hit the big limbs. Instead, he was raked with dozens of tiny branches. He managed to cover his face, but his arms felt as though they were being slashed by razors.

Somehow he kept his balance. He suddenly realized that the gravity was reversed on the top side of the disk. His feet were held in place, and he had only to turn his torso to direct the disk any way he wanted it to go.

He saw the startled aliens as he headed toward them. They quickly gained courage, however, when they saw he wasn't armed. Jack saw the paddle floating next to the canoe.

"T.J.," he shouted, "throw me the paddle."

T.J. reached for it, but an energy bolt singed his hand. In pain, he pulled his fingers back. But suddenly his other hand darted up, holding the pistol. He shot the nearest Visitor off his disk and grabbed the paddle at the same time. He held it up triumphantly, and Jack careered by the canoe, snapping it out of T.J.'s burned hand.

Two Visitors turned their disk toward him and came at him at full speed. Jack had been double-teamed before, and he knew what to do. He'd never had the pleasure of holding a canoe paddle in his hand when he played the Steelers, but, then, Pittsburgh didn't issue lasers to their players either.

As they approached, Jack held the paddle like a bat, as he had done before. But just when they were upon him, he turned it horizontally. As they were hit, the two Visitors emitted raspy groans and tumbled helplessly into the water.

There were only four or five of them now. If Jack could only get his hands on one of those laser guns . . .

Three of them surrounded the canoe. T.J. took aim at one of them, but the hammer clicked on an empty chamber. There was no time to reload.

Seeing T.J. in a hopeless position, Jack started toward the canoe to help. It was then that he saw perhaps twenty disk riders coming. Reinforcements.

As they approached him, Jack raised the paddle. A blue beam blasted it right out of his hands. The odor of burned wood in his nostrils, he struck out toward the oncoming alien troops and let fly with his fists as soon as he came close enough. An uppercut scored, knocking a Visitor off his disk and into another's arms. The second disk overturned with the extra mass, and both of them ended up in the drink.

Jack cut through their ranks like a buzz saw until he heard T.J. call his name.

One of the Visitors had his thinning hair in its claw. Another had a laser pistol against his temple. T.J. looked straight into Jack's eyes from thirty yards. "Get out of here while you've got the chance, Jack! Go!"

"If you try to escape, he will die," the leader of the marauding aliens said.

"Don't listen to him, Jack," T.J. shouted. "If you stay we'll both die."

"You have my word that you will be spared if you surrender."

Jack didn't believe him, but he couldn't risk letting T.J. die. "All right," he said softly.

"Return to your water craft," the Visitor commanded him.

Jack directed the disk toward the canoe and jumped in. The canoe rocked from side to side.

"You damn fool," T.J. said.

"If we go out," Jack said, "we go out together."

The Visitor said something in his own language. A disk floated out from behind the others. It was larger than any Jack had seen so far, and a strange device was mounted on the front that looked something like an architect's lamp. The Visitor riding the disk adjusted it until it was pointed right at the canoe.

"Here it comes, kid," T.J. said.

Violet waves poured out of the device. Jack turned his face away, hoping there would be no pain.

Chapter 15

"You don't suppose they got lost, do you?" Ham said.

"Not likely," Chris replied. "That sheriff's probably spent most of his life in these parts."

Ham shrugged. Chris didn't usually misunderstand his sarcasm, but this time it didn't matter much. Stern and Devereaux were two hours late, and it was getting dark. Ham was pretty sure the Visitors had them.

"Think we're gonna have to track them down too?" Chris said.

"Yeah. But if that sheriff got caught with his pants down out there, we better find somebody who knows his way around here real good."

"Right, Kemosabe."

They drove to the reservation, only half a mile away.

"Nice life the folks around here have," Ham remarked as they approached the recreation center. "Where the hell is the boss's hut?"

"This is the only public building here, Ham," Chris observed, "except for the school over there."

Ham noticed a tiny sign saying that Chief Martin Wooster's office was inside. He pulled up by the front door and got out. It was almost dark now, so he didn't have much chance of catching the chief at work. He tried the door anyway and found it locked.

He turned and shook his head. It was then that he noticed the four young men approaching. "Oh, shit," he muttered. "This is all we need."

They were swaggering. Chris got out of the Land-Rover and glared at them. They formed a semicircle around him and Ham.

"Come a little late to buy some beads," one of them said. He was a big man with broad shoulders and a sneer on his lip.

"That's not what we're looking for," Ham said.

"Maybe some Indian-head coconuts, then?"

"Nothing like that. We'd like to see the chief."

"Would you, now?" The group's spokesman shifted his weight menacingly, as though he would throw a punch at Ham.

Ham didn't flinch. "That's right, and it's pretty important."

"Yeah, I bet." Suddenly the spokesman swung his fist up at Ham's head. By the time it got there, Ham was gone. He pivoted on his left foot, bringing his cocked right leg up, lashing out with his right foot and screaming. He caught his assailant flush in the chest, heard him exhale every bit of wind in his lungs, turned him around, and shoved a knee in the small of his back while holding him in a half nelson.

The other three started toward him, but the click of Chris's .45 automatic dissuaded them. "Just stay cool," he said, "and stay healthy."

The three men backed away. Ham pushed their companion forward. "You boys aren't very neighborly, are you?"

A shot cracked through the muggy air like a thunderbolt.

"Drop it!" someone shouted from behind a shack.

Chris hesitated. Then he heard a click.

"Drop it, I said or so help me I'll blow you away."

A man wearing a cane hat stepped out into the open. He

carried a double-barreled 12-gauge shotgun as if he knew how to use it. "While you were thinking about it, I popped another shell into the chamber. Now I got two in this bird killer. One for each of you. You gonna drop it, now?"

"We didn't start this," Chris said.

The young man pointed his shotgun at Chris, asking the four Indians, "That true?"

None of them spoke.

"All right. Put that peashooter down, and I'll put the safety on this shotgun." He looked at the four youths contemptuously. "Why don't you boys take a powder."

Ham let go of the boy who had attacked him, and Chris holstered his weapon. The four youths backed away and vanished in the twilight shadows. As soon as they were gone, the two men's savior snapped the safety on and cradled the shotgun in both arms.

"How'd you know you could trust me?" he asked.

"You have an honest face," Ham said.

"You guys are professionals, aren't you?"

"That's right. I'm Tyler. That's Chris."

"I won't ask who you work for, just that you go away soon."

"You haven't told us who you are yet."

"My name is John Tiger."

"John Tiger . . . do you have a brother named Billy?" Ham asked.

John Tiger smiled wryly and shook his head. "Did that foolish sheriff put you on this?"

"Devereaux? No, we're not looking for your brother. Somebody else is missing."

"Always somebody missing in the swamp."

"Uh-hunh. We'd like to talk to the chief."

"He's a busy man."

"So am I," Ham said, "but I'm talking to you."

A glint of anger showed in John Tiger's eyes. "Don't do me any favors," he said.

"It's all right, John," said a white-haired man, walking toward them. "I'll talk to them."

"Chief Martin Wooster?" Ham said.

"Yeah."

"You may not like us, but when you find out who your new neighbors are here in the Everglades, even the 'gators are gonna seem like old friends."

Chapter 16

In her dream, Sabrina floated free in space. She drifted between planets as easily as one rolls over in bed. Each of the worlds she visited was beautiful, each different from all the others. At last she neared Earth, and it was the most beautiful planet of them all.

As Earth, planet of her birth, turned in the darkness, however, she noticed a subtle change occurring. The white striations of clouds masked a transformation, a mottling and darkening of the blue seas. They became green and coarse, hardening, ridges forming on them. Like lizard skin. Sabrina was horrified to see such a horrid transmogrification. She tried to cry out, but she couldn't make a sound. She was sinking into Earth's gravity well, and she couldn't stop. Squamous, green appendages grew out of the North American continent. They formed talons, reaching for her. She was falling right into them.

They closed over her as she tumbled into them.

She opened her eyes.

Dr. Morrow stood over her. He wore his human makeup, as always.

"What do you want?" she demanded.

"I heard you cry out," Dr. Morrow said, "so I came in to see if I could help."

Sabrina sighed. Sitting up, she reached for a flask of water on the table by her bed. "You can help me by letting me go. Until you do that, I see no reason why I should talk to you."

"You *will* talk to me, my dear Dr. Fontaine—one way or another."

Sabrina slammed the flask down on the table. "Was that a threat?"

"Call it whatever you like, but you will talk."

"Do you intend to put me in a conversion chamber, Dr. Morrow?"

"If necessary."

"If that's the case, you defeat your own purpose."

"What do you know of my purpose?" His face was blank, his sunglasses reflecting two tiny images of her angry expression.

"I know that you need me." She knew no such thing, but the statement was worth risking if she could learn if it was true.

"What makes you think so?"

"Why would you go to the trouble of luring me here otherwise?"

"Haven't you heard that we like to dispose of scientists?" Dr. Morrow asked dryly.

"Yes, I've heard that." Sabrina spoke calmly, sensing that Morrow was evading the real issue. "But you're badly understaffed here, and your research is rather urgent. That's why you've kidnapped me and the others."

"You know about the others?"

"Of course," she lied.

"Very well," Dr. Morrow said after a few moments of deep thought. "We'll give you a little more time to come to your senses, Dr. Fontaine. But not much more time. You will be converted if you cannot see the value of working with us willingly. That would be a pity."

"Yes, it would be, particularly if you destroy my mind," Sabrina responded coolly. "Then I would be of no use to you at all."

"*If* the process destroys your mind. There is a good chance that no such thing would happen."

"I'm quite sure that I would not succumb," Sabrina said confidently.

Dr. Morrow stepped into the doorway as it opened. He turned and pointed a finger at her. "Don't be too certain, Dr. Fontaine, and don't be too certain that I won't be willing to convert you if all else fails."

He walked out. Just as the door was closing, Sabrina heard the same terrible scream she had heard a day or two before.

She shrank back into her cell, wanting to cry but refusing to permit herself to show any emotion. They were watching, but they would see no sign of weakness in her.

Chapter 17

The coffee was perking in Chief Martin Wooster's humble office. Marie Whitley had joined them there at the chief's request, and she was clearly distraught.

"Sheriff Devereaux was trying to help, and now he's gone too," she said. "What can be causing this?"

"Something most people would like to believe is a thing of the past," Ham said.

"I don't understand," Marie said.

"Well, it's the same way people talk about Nazis nowadays, like they were some aberration in the past that can never return. But they weren't," Ham explained. "They were people like you and me who got caught up in something bigger than they were. Maybe a lot of them sensed it was wrong, but it was powerful and they were just ordinary people. What could they do but go along with it?"

"I still don't understand."

"What I'm trying to say is that the Visitors are still here."

"The Visitors? I thought—"

"You thought they were all gone. But they're not gone. At least not all of them. Some of them are hiding right here in the Everglades."

"How do you know this?" Chief Wooster asked.

"Just between you and me and the coffeepot, Chief, I've been involved in a lot of intelligence operations. Chris and I have both ferreted out a lot of espionage agents. This thing has got a smell about it. Somebody very powerful is behind these disappearances, somebody not of this earth."

"But what makes you so sure?"

"Who could it be besides the Visitors? Cubans? Russians? It's not the way they operate."

"Suppose you're right," Marie said. "We still don't understand why they're kidnapping people—"she turned grim—"or killing them."

"My guess is," Ham said as he poured himself a cup of coffee, "that they need people for some kind of labor. Some of the work they're doing is very specialized. Biological. We must assume that they've already developed an antitoxin."

"Granted, if they're still here," Martin said.

"If they've got that under their belts, they're free to develop their own strain of bacteria that would be harmless to them but which could kill humans."

"Thus reversing our roles," Marie murmured.

"And that's only one of many possibilities. Don't forget, these lizards are centuries ahead of us in most respects. They can travel from Sirius to Earth, develop a cure for cancer, create a human disguise so good that we can't detect it—and they've succeeded in mating one of their species with one of ours."

"The star child, Elizabeth," Marie said, wonder in her voice.

"Then, you don't believe the Visitors have given up on their plans of world conquest, Mr. Tyler?" Chief Wooster asked.

"No, of course I don't. They need the water—and the food."

Marie shuddered, thinking of what they might have done to Billy by now.

"What can we do, Mr. Tyler?" she asked.

"You can help us fight them," Ham said, "or you can sit back and let them take over the way so many did in Europe back in the thirties."

"I'll help you."

"Now, just a minute, Marie," Chief Wooster said. "You don't know that these men are right. You don't even know that they're who they say they are."

"I don't care," Marie said defiantly. "I want Billy back, and these men are the only ones who have given me any hope so far. Everyone around here would rather pretend nothing's happened."

"Nobody's pretending, Marie. It's just that we prefer to deal with problems ourselves, rather than having CIA men come in and tell us what to do."

"Is it better to have half the tribe disappear than to let these men help?" Marie asked. "Pride can only go so far, and then you have to start being practical."

"A lot of people suspect the government may be behind our problems," Martin said. "Just as they have been so many times in the past."

"Why would they kidnap people out here?" Ham interjected.

"Why would you, you mean," the chief said, shooting Ham an angry look. "*You* are the government, Mr. Tyler. How can we trust you after all that's happened? How do we really know you're here to help us?"

"They're not here to help," a voice said from the doorway. They all turned to see John Tiger enter the cramped office.

"What do you mean?" the chief asked.

"They're here because they need our help."

The chief and Marie stared at Ham and Chris.

"What are you trying to say?" Ham asked after an awkward few seconds of silence.

"I heard some things in the swamp today. Shots and other noises. After things quieted down, I went out where all the commotion had come from. I found an upended canoe—and a paddle that was divided in two pieces."

"Broken?"

"No—burned in two."

Chris whistled.

"They got 'em, all right," Ham said. "Just like they got Billy Tiger, Walter Miles, and all the others."

"So that just leaves the two of you, doesn't it?" John observed. "And the two of you may be tough, but you can't go up against them all alone."

"You want us to beg?" Ham asked. "Is that it?"

"I don't want you to do anything except go back to Miami or Washington or wherever it is you came from and leave us alone."

"Are you crazy? You know what's going on out here. How can you just turn your back on it?"

"I'll fight them in my own way, with my own people. What do you say, Martin."

The chief ran a weathered hand through his snow-white shock of hair. "I guess that's the way I feel about it too, Johnny."

Marie stood and faced John Tiger, fire in her eyes. "He's your brother!" she shouted at him. "These men can help us, and you let your pride stand in the way."

"Do you know what people like them do to our brothers and sisters in Central America?" John said from between clenched teeth. "They'll use us and throw us away if it suits them, because they don't even think we're human."

With that, he stormed out of the office. They heard his boots echoing in the hallway until he was gone from the building.

Marie turned to Ham and Chris. "I don't care. I'll help you."

"Thanks," he replied. "We're gonna need it, just like he said." Ham turned to Chief Martin Wooster. "How about you, Chief?"

The chief took a sip of coffee, made a sour face, and said, "John's a little hot under the collar. His father was the same way. Still, he did say some things that are true."

"Does this mean you're not with us?" Ham asked.

"I'm with you," he said. "At least for the time being, but I can't guarantee how the rest of the tribe will feel about this."

"You'll talk to them, then?"

"I'll talk to them." The chief poured them all another cup of coffee.

Chapter 18

"It isn't much of a plan," Jack said, "but it's the only one we've got."

T.J. nodded. Ever since they had awakened in this double cell, they had been noting every detail of their captors' behavior. When their jailer brought in food, they had decided, was their best chance to get out. Once they overpowered him and got outside the door, they would have no idea where they were, but at least they would be free and fighting back.

They had been strangely lethargic during the first few hours of consciousness, a state they attributed to the device that had been trained on them in the swamp. They had only regained their senses fully in the past few hours. Neither of them had any idea of how much time had passed since their capture, but they agreed that it was probably more than twenty-four hours.

"I know Sabrina's here," Jack said, stretching his muscles. "If—when—we get out that door, I'm going to find her."

T.J. nodded. "We'll see what we can do about that, but let's just see about getting out of this mousetrap first."

T.J. scoured the cell for something heavy to use as a weapon. The objects available were solid and durable, but as light as balsa wood. The table they ate from looked as if it would weigh at least twenty pounds, but it was as light as a feather. T.J. scowled in disgust.

"I guess they know us well enough to realize we'd use this stuff against them," he said. "So they gave us stuff that couldn't hurt a fly."

"They forgot about these," Jack said, holding out his hands.

"I was pretty good with my fists at one time," T.J. said, "but it's been awhile."

As T.J. flexed his sausage fingers, the door slid open. A Visitor, wearing no makeup, stood on the threshold with a tray of food. Jack and T.J. tried to pretend disinterest, as they had planned. It worked. The Visitor entered without hesitation as soon as he had pocketed his crystal key.

Jack let him walk a little bit past him, then he leaped over a chair and punched him at the base of his horny head.

The alien's forked tongue shot out of his mouth, then he groaned and sagged to the floor. Jack bent over the fallen Visitor as T.J. rushed to the door.

"What are you doin', Jack?" he said. "Come on."

"Just a second, T.J." Jack searched the Visitor's body, sidestepping the viscous blobs of blue-green food on the floor. He felt something in a pocket that was smooth and hard edged. "I've got it," he said, pulling the crystal key out and holding it up. He picked up the food tray and stood up.

"If you don't hurry it up," T.J. said, "we'll both get it . . . right between the eyes."

They were off and running. T.J. moved fast for a man of his size. They sprinted down a corridor, turning a corner. A Visitor was walking right toward them. For a moment he just stopped and stared, his yellow eyes intent on them. Then he pulled his laser pistol and took aim.

Jack jumped in front of T.J. Holding the tray in front of him, he crouched and rushed headlong at the alien. The plastic tray sizzled and a half-inch-wide hole opened near its center, emitting a blue energy bolt that narrowly missed Jack's head. A second shot burned a corner of the tray, and a third made a U-shaped hole in its bottom. Jack danced back and forth in the corridor like a broken-field runner chased by the entire Green Bay defense.

He held little more than a saucer-sized, dripping blob of melting plastic by the time he was close enough to strike.

The alien was about to fire the shot that would finally bring Jack down when Jack let out a bloodcurdling scream and pitched the smoking plastic at him like a baseball.

It hit the Visitor in the shoulder, some of the burning plastic clinging to his crimson uniform. He hissed and tried to brush it away. Afraid to burn his claw, he flailed away at it with the barrel of his pistol.

Jack was on him then. He lashed out with his right hand, feeling the leathery flesh and the resisting reptilian jaw beneath it. The Visitor was knocked off his feet, landing on the corridor floor shoulders first.

"Good night," Jack said, taking the laser pistol from the unconscious creature.

T.J. was right behind him. "Better keep moving, Jack," he said. He glanced down at the alien. "Nice punch."

"Thanks."

They started running again, turning another corner without seeing anyone, and then another. As they moved along through the third such passageway, Jack noticed that the light was dimming. He remembered that the Visitors didn't see well in bright light. This could be one of their work areas. He held up a hand for T.J. to stop, and he peered around a corner, through a latticework bulkhead.

He saw a Visitor working a beam like the one they had used on him and T.J. But he wasn't using it on a human. He was putting an alligator to sleep with it. A big alligator, maybe fifteen feet long. It was in a tank, and behind it were hundreds of other such tanks. They all contained reptiles—not just alligators, but snakes, lizards, and who knew what else. They were like specimens in a lab back at the university.

The Visitor massaged the 'gator with the violet waves until it was out cold. It almost looked as though it were smiling, its huge, crooked jaws turning up behind the eyes in a pleased expression.

A larger machine floated in with a man riding on it. He was positioned in a seat behind a curving console, working a device with a long, sinuous appendage that opened into an oblong cavity.

The machine began to whir, and Jack saw green sparks inside the dark cavity. The water in the sleeping 'gator's tank roiled as if the gator was stirring, but he hadn't budged.

The water began to spout upward, but it didn't spill over the side, even when it was over the open top of the glass tank. Everything inside suddenly started to float upward—the 'gator as well as the huge blob of dirty water. When it was positioned in front of the machine, the entire apparatus—driver, 'gator, water and all—glided silently into an exit resembling a big hangar door.

"What do you think is behind that door?" Jack asked.

"You may not want to know," a voice said, "once you find out."

It wasn't T.J.'s voice. Jack whipped around. T.J. was still there, but a scaly hand held a laser pistol against his head.

Chapter 19

Thorkel entered Dr. Morrow's quarters for the first time. The great scientist's rooms were dimly lit by a revolving light sculpture of changing hues. Dr. Thorkel was always calmed by this mode of Visitor expression, and he supposed they must have found it restful too.

The door shut behind him. Dr. Morrow sat at a desk, facing him as he walked past the fascinating sculpture, its colors reflected in his dark glasses.

"Dr. Thorkel," he said. "So good of you to come."

He always admired the Visitors' manners, particularly those of Dr. Morrow. They were the hallmark of a truly civilized race. "It is my pleasure."

"Doctor, our work on the prototype has reached a point where theory is no longer enough. Don't you agree?" Dr. Morrow leaned back in his chair and pressed his fingertips together in front of his chest.

"I'm not sure I understand," Thorkel said.

"Please sit down." Dr. Morrow indicated a chair opposite him.

Thorkel sat down. He looked across the desk at Dr. Morrow,

watching the colored lights play across his face and gleam on the curve of his dark glasses.

"The ability of the prototype must be tested, don't you agree?" Dr. Morrow said.

"Of course. How else can we ever know if it will be effective?"

"Precisely. We must know how it will respond to stimulus in the field—a controlled experiment, you might say."

"I agree that this should be our next step in this program," Dr. Thorkel said, running his fingers through the thin hair on the back of his bald head. "But what will we test the prototype against?"

Dr. Morrow smiled. "Suppose you leave that to me, Dr. Thorkel?"

There was something in Dr. Morrow's tone that made him uneasy. For the first time it crossed his mind that he was being used. He quickly squelched the thought, certain that it was nonproductive. "I'll be very interested in seeing what you have in mind."

"I knew you would be," Dr. Morrow said. "In a way, this will be a test for you too, Dr. Thorkel."

"For . . . me?"

Dr. Morrow laughed, a rasping, hissing sound that was totally nonhuman.

Unable to sleep, Billy got out of bed and paced the floor of his tiny cell. They had stopped taking the tissue samples, so he was visited only half as often as before. The only time the cell door opened now, it was to admit someone bringing food for him.

That meant two things. They didn't need him for their experiments any longer, and he had better make his escape attempt very soon.

He was getting hungry now, so they should be coming soon. If he didn't do it now, he never would.

Positioning himself by the door, he waited.

Somewhere between thirty minutes and an hour passed

before the door whooshed open. Billy crouched, ready to spring on the jailer.

But the jailer wasn't alone. There were two others with him, both training laser pistols right at Billy. The jailer didn't carry a food tray. Instead, he had something that looked like a big desk lamp. He pointed it at Billy.

"What are you doing?" Billy cried. This couldn't be happening. This was the moment he was going to make his break for freedom.

A chirping sound came out of the strange device. Violet waves shot toward him. Billy tried to jump out of the way, but the waves fanned out through the room. He was caught in the waves, but they didn't burn him, as he expected, nor did they hurt him in any way. They immersed him, bathing him in their warmth, soothing him, calming his fears.

Soon he was almost asleep. The jailer came into the cell and took him by the elbow.

Billy was gently led away.

Chapter 20

"Don't get too far away," Ham called to Chris and Martin from the canoe. "Try to stay within earshot, if not in sight."

Ham paddled as Marie sat near the prow as lookout.

"Look at this stuff," he said, watching the water drip from the end of his oar. "We take it for granted, and the Visitors have come eight or ten light-years just to wet their claws in it."

"It seems odd that it's such a rare thing on other planets," Marie said.

"From what I understand, hydrogen is the most common element in the universe. It's oxygen that's rare, and you need both hydrogen and oxygen for water."

"Well, if they're here in the swamp, they've got all the water they could ever want."

"For a few of them, yes," Ham agreed. "But not for an entire race, and then there's their protein shortage."

Marie shuddered. She'd seen a 'gator eat a small dog when she was a girl; that was the image that popped into her mind when she thought of the Visitors eating mammals.

"From what John Tiger told Martin," Ham said, shipping

his oar, "it was right around here that he found the burned paddle."

"I don't see anything." Marie squinted as sunlight found its way through the thick foliage.

"John must have taken the paddle." Ham began to row again, keeping his eyes peeled for any signs of a struggle. They drifted silently for a moment, and then he saw something.

"Look at that cypress tree," he said.

"Which one?"

"The big one in the middle, on the bank with those other cypresses."

Marie squinted again, and then she saw it. "The trunk is burned."

"In a couple of places. This is where they took Stern and Devereaux. I'd put money on it."

They moved closer to the trees.

"They must have come from this direction," Ham said, Pointing past the embankment. "From deep in the swamp."

"People don't go in there," Marie said. "They never have."

"Sounds ominous," Ham responded. "Why don't they go that way?"

"It's very treacherous, a lot of dead wood to snag you, thick with 'gators, diamondbacks, you name it. If it's bad, it's in there."

"Just the place for our slimy friends to hang out."

"Yeah, I guess it would be easier for them to stay hidden back there, all right," Marie said. "But how could they survive in such a place?"

"Are you kidding? To those erect lizards, it's probably just like Miami Beach," Ham said, fishing two abandoned laser guns out of the water.

John Tiger set his paddle against the huge banyan root protruding from the water and pushed off. He knew the rest of the fallen tree was under there, and he had no desire to have the bottom of his canoe ripped out by another root.

He hoped the two CIA men were off in some other part of

the swamp, because he suspected that Marie and Martin were with them. He didn't want them anywhere near this place, now more than ever. If the Visitors were here, there would be a way to deal with them, and he didn't want a girl and an old man around to mess things up.

Passing within three yards of a 'gator sunning itself on a log, John stopped paddling. From here on in, he didn't want to make a sound. He remembered once when he and Billy were kids, ten or twelve years ago, they took a canoe in here. The old man had spanked the shit out of them because it was so dangerous. Because of that, neither of them had ever come back here, even as men. But John recalled one big mud flat stretching for hundreds of yards. He suspected that was where the alien encampment would be.

If he remembered correctly, it was right around here. John parted some fronds, and there it was.

Gleaming white towers rose out of the mud, connecting walls on which sentries walked back and forth. He couldn't see them clearly from here, but they were wearing red uniforms. On the towers, machines were pointed toward the sky. Trees seemed to be floating in the air, an illusion created by projections from the machines.

The Visitors had paved over the mud flat and built their compound here. Tyler was right.

John watched them for a while, trying to decide what to do. Should he wait until nightfall, break in, and try to find his brother? Or should he go back and get reinforcements?

He backed the canoe out of the narrow space between a dead tree and a muddy bank when one of the fronds burst into flame. it sputtered and went out, leaving only the charred tip of the stem.

John started paddling, the high-pitched whine of lasers all around him. They were firing at him from the towers, so they had a long way to go before they caught up with him. He sliced through the water, heart beating wildly.

Between strokes, he began to hear a low hum. He glanced over his shoulder to see a Visitor coming after him on an antigravity disk. No, not just one disk, three or four. In a moment, the sky would be full of them.

As the first one drew near, John leaped out of the canoe and dodged the laser fire. The mud at his feet bubbled, but he didn't even slow down.

If he could get to where the foliage was so thick they couldn't see him, he had a chance.

The Visitor's shadow was right next to him as he ran, blue beams missing him narrowly. The other Visitors were way behind this eager beaver. If he could ditch this one, he was pretty sure he could make it.

He felt the heat of an energy beam that passed within an inch of his face. Nevertheless, he slowed his pace. He heard the Visitor's lizard tongue click in satisfaction.

John looked over his shoulder to see the disk coming lower. Suddenly, he sprinted forward into the shade of an enormous banyan tree.

The Visitor changed direction to follow him, failing to see the thick limb that hit him in the head. John heard him gasp, and then a splash. But he never looked back to see his fallen foe.

He just kept running into the thickets, deeper and deeper into the swamp.

Chapter 21

Soon after Jack and T.J. were back in their cells, the Visitors came and dragged them both out and down a long corridor. At last a key was inserted, a door slid open, and they were breathing fresh air for the first time in days.

"Gonna feed us to the 'gators," T.J. said, "or eat us themselves?"

Jack caught a glimpse of what looked like a theater. Row on row of curving seats rose almost to the top of the walls. They were filled with Visitors, hundreds of them without human makeup.

T.J. was pushed forward into the arena, but the door slammed shut and Jack was roughly pulled away. He was dragged up a ramp, at the end of which was a cubicle with a one-way pane of glass looking out onto the arena. He saw T.J., looking bewildered, standing near one wall.

A niche opened behind him, and a Visitor stepped out. He held out T.J.'s .38, holster and all. T.J. accepted it, examined it quickly, and strapped the gun belt onto his ample middle.

The crowd clucked and hissed and then became subdued, as if anticipating something.

At the far end of the arena, a door opened from the bottom. Jack saw nothing at first, but then he caught a movement in the shadows. Something emerged that was like a nightmare come to life.

"No!" Jack gasped. They had put T.J. in the arena with a monster. The thing stood eight or nine feet tall on its hind legs. Its hands and feet were huge, clawed talons, its skin scaly and thick like armor plating.

Its face was horrible. A long snout with teeth like yellow spikes protruded from a cranium that was shaped like a man's. The eyes were unmistakably human, though set back on the horny, saurian head. They glared malevolently at T.J. now, the creature advancing across the dusty arena floor, its eight-foot tail lashing behind it.

T.J. was frozen to the spot where he had first set eyes on the monstrous reptile man. He wondered if they had really brought him here, or if he were still lying asleep in his cell, dreaming.

The crowd began to roar and cheer as though they were Romans at the Circus Maximus. Jack watched them through the one-way glass with such hatred and contempt that he almost didn't see Sabrina for a moment.

She was there in the stands with two other humans—at least, they looked like humans. Two middle-aged men sat on either side of her, one balding, the other white-haired and bearded. As the beast man closed in on T.J., Sabrina buried her face in her hands.

At least he knew she was alive—and he was near her.

"Most ingenious, don't you agree?" Dr. Morrow asked. "We have successfully combined the genetic materials of a human and a swamp-dwelling, amphibious reptile. Dr. Thorkel was instrumental in achieving the magnificent result of the recombinant DNA experiment you see before you."

Sabrina looked away. "It's horrible," she said.

"I had hoped you would say that."

"How could you help to produce such a hideous thing?" Sabrina asked Dr. Thorkel.

"Dr. Fontaine," Thorkel protested weakly, "nothing like this has ever been done on Earth before. Surely you can see that—"

"That you are a traitor to the human race," she spat. "Yes, I can see that, all right."

"Come, come," Dr. Morrow said, "let us watch the spectacle now."

T.J. had seen 'gators before, but this was like something that might show up after a toot on half a gallon of bad moonshine. He wanted to believe it wasn't real, but the dust and sweat in his mouth, the sun beating down on the back of his neck, the heft of the .38 in his hand all told him it was.

Well, at least he had the gun. 'Gators had been shot to death by pistols before. He wished to God he had a good rifle, because he was going to have to let that ugly sucker get awful close before he dared waste any ammunition on it.

"Come on, you son of a bitch," T.J. said. "Come a little closer." His damp fingers flipped the safety off and cocked the hammer. "Just come on."

The monster opened its enormous jaws and howled a terrible challenge that was neither human nor reptile, but a hellish combination of the two.

The short hairs on the back of T.J.'s neck stood on end. He didn't want it near him. He had six shots; maybe if he fired one, he would scare it away even if he missed.

Feet spread wide apart, T.J. gripped the revolver firmly in both hands. He let the thing come a little bit closer until he was certain he had drawn a bead on it. He aimed for the middle of its chest. That way, he'd almost certainly hit one or more of the vital organs.

T.J. squeezed off a shot, his beefy arms jerking back. The deafening roar of the pistol shut out the sound of the audience.

The monster moved spasmodically but remained standing.

"Good shot, ole boy," T.J. congratulated himself.

He waited for it to fall, but then, with growing alarm, he saw what had happened. There was a dent in the armor-plated breast of the creature, nothing more. The bullet hadn't even penetrated its thick hide, let alone struck a vital organ.

The monster looked down at the insignificant mark on its massive chest and then threw back its head and roared.

As it began moving toward T.J. once more, the crowd cheered enthusiastically.

Chapter 22

"You've proven your point," Dr. Thorkel said. "It's impervious to gunfire. Don't you think it's time to put a stop to this carnival?"

Sabrina looked at Thorkel in surprise. Perhaps he saw the truth at last.

"Please don't be squeamish, Dr. Thorkel," said Dr. Morrow. "We have only learned how strong its armor is. Now we'll see how efficient it is at killing."

"No!" Sabrina cried. "Please don't do this."

But Dr. Morrow turned his attention back to the two figures below as the crowd hissed its approval.

This time T.J. waited until the thing was closer before firing. He aimed for the head. When he was sure he couldn't miss, he shot the creature for the second time.

The reptile man's head snapped back. Involuntarily holding his breath, T.J. waited for it to fall. It rolled its head back and forth on its thick neck, staggered, but then threw its shoulders back and emitted a staccato sound that might have been laughter.

"I hit that goddamn thing flush in the skull," T.J. muttered.

The monster started toward him again from not more than four yards away. T.J. knew that his only chance was to shoot out its eyes. That was going to take some fancy shooting.

Suddenly the monster's speed increased. It rushed T.J. just like a 'gator on two legs. He fired at its belly, just to give himself a chance to move out of its way.

T.J.'s ankle turned and he slammed into the dusty ground. Rolling over, he saw the scaly thing changing direction to pounce on him. It opened its mouth to roar, and he fired.

The bullet struck the soft tissue on the roof its mouth. The monster shrieked horribly, its clawed hands cupping its snout in a very human gesture.

Getting off the ground hurt his ankle, but T.J. managed it. He ran toward the opposite wall. There were two bullets left in his revolver. He would have to make them count.

The reptile man shook its massive head, blood streaming from its jaws. Apparently the bullet had only effected a flesh wound.

Two bullets left. He had to hit it in the eye at least once or he was finished. There was still a chance he could blind the thing, but even one bullet might be enough if it went through the eye and penetrated the brain. The monster charged at him. T.J. had never wanted to get away from something so badly in his entire life, but he stood his ground nevertheless.

It was less than the length of T.J.'s shadow away, perhaps five feet, when he fired his fifth shot. It ricocheted off the bony ridge just over its left eye, enraging it even further.

It rushed at him headfirst, its flailing tail sending up clouds of dust behind it.

T.J. waited until he could smell its fetid stench, and still he didn't shoot. Its huge, webbed talons reached out for him, but its head was still down. T.J. couldn't get a shot at either eye.

Despairing, he still didn't squeeze the trigger. The monster seized him by the waist and lifted him bodily off the ground.

"Jesus," he moaned. It wasn't a curse, but a prayer. He felt his ribs cracking, heard his bones breaking, and knew he was going to die. All he wanted now was to take this horror with him.

The crowd's wildly enthusiastic cheers rang in his ears as he lifted the pistol painfully toward the monster's head.

It turned its head to get a better look at him, the humanoid eye on the right side of its lumpy cranium blinking.

Now. T.J. lifted his hand the last few inches, his fingers numb and trembling. *Now*.

The grotesque creature hurled him onto the arena floor. T.J. landed in bone-crushing pain, and yet he somehow still gripped the pistol.

He tried to crawl away as the beast's right claw reached out for him, but his body wouldn't respond to his will. Was his spine broken?

The talons grasped him by the throat and pulled him off the ground. T.J. tasted hot blood in his mouth. He became dizzy, white motes dancing in front of his eyes. Darkness was coming, but he could still lift his arm, however slowly.

Now the monster faced him straight on as it held him near its hideous jaws. T.J. could swear it was grinning at him, its horrid maw gaping to expose the dagger teeth. Saliva gushed from its mouth.

The pistol was in position as the thing cocked its head for a better look again. T.J. shoved the snubnosed barrel at the eye, willing himself to shoot.

Before he could squeeze the trigger, his wrist was caught in a viselike grip. Horrified, he saw the scaly tail wrapping itself around his arm so tightly that all sensation was cut off.

"Squeeze!" he commanded his finger.

The saurian head seemed to be laughing at him as his life was drained out of his dying body. Still, T.J. tried to shoot. He knew he could do it if he could just line up the eye in his sight once more.

There! There it was. All he had to do was pull the trigger.

With its free claw, the monster slapped the gun out of T.J.'s hand as easily as a child might swat a fly. The last thing T.J. ever heard was the .38's report as it went off harmlessly in the air.

Chapter 23

"How horrible," Sabrina sobbed. She wept openly at the sight of the poor man's death. Dr. Thorkel patted her arm, trying to comfort her. "Perhaps now," she said to him, "you'll believe that the Visitors don't have our best interests at heart."

"I'm sorry, Dr. Fontaine," he said. "I'm so sorry."

"Please spare me the sentimentality," Dr. Morrow said. "You humans are far too emotional for your own good."

"It's too much," Dr. Thorkel said. "You never said there would be anything like this." He gestured at the bloodthirsty crowd as they screeched and hissed behind the three of them. "You never said you would use the prototype to kill innocent human beings."

"Are you really such a fool, Dr. Thorkel, that it never occurred to you that we were creating this living fighting machine for some other purpose besides pure research?" Dr. Morrow smiled in a mockery of human pleasure that made Sabrina want to tear the mask from his face and expose him for the reptilian creature that he was. "We have succeeded beyond your wildest dreams in recombining human and reptile genes, haven't we?"

"But how could it withstand those bullets?" Thorkel asked, too much the scientist to ignore such an intriguing question, even at a time like this.

"Something we added to the mixture, Dr. Thorkel. A molecular density that protects the creature even as it makes him stronger and more agile."

"Incredible," Dr. Thorkel said.

"Does it make you feel like the inferior ape you are, Doctor?" Morrow asked. "You humans amaze me. You think, with your primitive science, that you can defeat us. We have suffered a temporary setback, it is true, but we have the knowledge to destroy you all. We would have preferred doing it differently, of course. It would have been so much less trouble to simply rule over your pathetic species as we originally planned. You give us no choice now but to fight you. And we *will* break your spirit, Dr. Fontaine, just as we will break the spirit of all humankind."

"You'll never defeat us," Sabrina said with steel in her voice.

"Oh, no?" Dr. Morrow signaled a crew of technicians to clear the arena. Then they turned a tripod-mounted globular device on the monster.

The monster stopped eating when it felt the tractor beam pushing against it. It tried to withstand the powerful force, but even its great strength was no use against the alien device. It was soon safely behind the door again.

A few seconds later, another door opened in the arena wall.

"Haven't you spilled enough blood for one day?" Sabrina demanded.

"My dear Dr. Fontaine," Morrow said. "The prototype has only passed its first test. The subject did very well against a rather sluggish member of your race."

"That poor man fought bravely."

"Yes, but we would like to find out how the prototype will do against a fine physical specimen—an athlete."

Dr. Morrow gesticulated, and two sentries appeared in the dark aperture on the far side of the arena. Between them was a third figure, yet another sentry behind him, holding a laser pistol at his head. He towered over all three of them, his blond hair blowing in the breeze. Sabrina's heart pounded wildly as she saw him.

"I think this one is just the right adversary for our little creation, wouldn't you agree?"

"No." She must have been hallucinating.

Dr. Morrow slyly watched her. "No? But why not, Dr. Fontaine? Surely you have no special interest in such an oaf?"

"How did you bring him here? Why?" Tears were streaming down her cheeks.

"He came looking for you. Curious behavior for one of your gladiators, I'd say."

Sabrina recalled how her colleagues had made such jokes about Jack. Jock, ape, muscle-bound clod, they had called him. But none of them had really known him. He was intelligent and, in spite of his profession, gentle. She had thought about him often since she had been trapped here, but she never thought he would be able to track her down.

"Do you know this man, Dr. Fontaine?" Thorkel asked.

"Yes," Sabrina said, wiping away her tears. "Yes, I know him."

There was no use in trying to hide it. Her reaction had given her feelings for Jack away the moment she had seen him, if there had ever been any doubt in Morrow's mind to begin with.

Jack stood proudly in the center of the arena now. He showed no fear in spite of what he had just seen. He had considered T. J. Devereaux a friend, even though they had only known one another for a short time. T.J. would not have died in vain if Jack could help it.

"Sabrina," he said in a clear voice, "I love you."

"Jack!" she cried. She started out of her seat, but Dr. Morrow's hand on her arm restrained her. She could have broken free of his grip, but she was afraid it would go worse for Jack if she did.

Dr. Morrow dismissed those remaining in the arena with an imperious wave of his hand. Jack was taken away, stealing one last glance at Sabrina before the door in the arena wall closed behind him.

"Yes," Dr. Morrow said, "he will do very well in the experimental combat arena. I'm certain of it."

"Is there . . ." Sabrina could hardly speak, she was so choked with emotion.

"Did you say something, Dr. Fontaine?"

"Is there . . . any way that you could use another combatant—perhaps a nonhuman one?"

"Nonhuman—a very interesting idea," Dr. Morrow mused, "but not a very practical one. No, we must have a human, I'm afraid."

Sabrina was ashamed to be begging, even for Jack's life. She had no choice, though.

"If you must have a human," she said, "can you . . ."

"Can I what, Dr. Fontaine?"

"Can you make it someone else besides Jack?"

"Ah, you want me to do you a favor." Morrow stared at her through his dark glasses. "And what are you prepared to do for me in return?"

Sabrina sighed. "I'll do anything you ask," she said meekly.

"Good," he said, smiling. "Then we understand one another."

She nodded, wiping away her tears with the back of her hand. Just as Dr. Morrow had predicted, she was beaten. She would work for him.

But at least she had saved Jack's life.

Chapter 24

Like a wild animal, John Tiger had lived in the thick growth of the swamp, eating berries and a snake he had killed. He was slowly working his way back to the reservation by an indirect route. He wasn't going to be caught out in the open, no matter what. It troubled him that Billy would have to wait for help while he backtracked, but he wouldn't be able to do much if they captured him. He had to stay free if Billy was to have a chance.

His clothes torn and dirty, John crouched as he made his way through a stand of palmettos. Suddenly he stopped moving, hearing voices.

A frog croaked near him. A mosquito buzzed by his face, but he didn't slap at it. He lay flat on his stomach in the mud.

The voices came closer, and there was another sound accompanying them: the soft splash of paddles striking water. Were they human? Perhaps—and perhaps not. The Visitors could have adopted this mode of swamp travel to look for him.

The voices came closer still, gaining clarity. They sounded like men's voices, speaking in low voices. And then he heard a woman's higher tones.

Marie.

John fought his way out through the thistles and thorns. "Marie!" he shouted. He could see them, Marie and some men in canoes, as they rounded an old dead tree whose branches stretched out of the water like the hand of a skeleton. The two CIA men were with her, and Martin was leading them!

"Martin! It's me, John Tiger!"

They looked up and saw him as he splashed waist-high into the water.

"Johnny!" Marie cried. "Watch out for 'gators."

"Get back on land, John," Martin called out to him. "We'll be there in a minute, son."

The big CIA man started paddling toward him, but John didn't follow Martin's advice. He waded through the lily pads to meet them.

"I found their camp," he told them breathlessly. "But they saw me, and they've been chasing me ever since."

"Come on now, boy," Martin said. He reached out to pull John in. "There's not much room in here for three, but I guess we'll manage somehow."

John was in water up to his chest now. He couldn't have been more than four feet from the canoe. He raised his hand and surged forward. Martin's powerful fingers grasped his and began to pull him out of the water.

A blue flash blinded John for a moment. At first he thought it was the sun reflected off the water, but then he smelled the terrible odor of burned flesh.

Martin was staring straight into his eyes. In his chest was a smoking hole through which John could see daylight.

Martin tried to speak, but he couldn't. He slumped over, a hand dangling in the water. John still held the other hand in his own.

"Martin." He had known this man all his life. He was like a relative. He couldn't just die like this.

Blue beams crisscrossed the air behind the canoe, but John didn't move. He just held on to Martin's hand.

"Johnny!" Marie cried from the other canoe.

Tyler was with her. He pulled out a laser gun and fired at a

Visitor coming in low on an antigravity disk. The Visitor was hit in the head. He went into the water, yowling in pain.

Chris was firing too. He burned the pins out from another one. One disk after another sliced into the water.

As another flew in over them, Marie fired a .410 shotgun at him. She didn't hit him, since he was almost directly overhead, but the blast flipped his antigravity disk neatly over and dumped him in with his companions.

She blew another one off his disk a moment later. John watched her and the other two fighting, but it didn't seem real. Only when he saw the Visitor coming up behind her did he take action.

Chris was busy firing in the other direction as John leaped into the canoe and dived from there onto the disk. He caught the Visitor by the legs, but he didn't succeed in toppling him.

The alien fell to his hands and knees, John's torso sprawled across the disk under his chest. The creature fumbled with his laser pistol, trying to get off a shot.

John drew his knife out. Just as the Visitor trained his laser on him, John plunged the knife into his guts.

Black lips drew back from the Visitor's fanged mouth, and blue-green ichor spilled onto John's hand. He tossed the body off the disk and stood proudly on it in the Visitor's place.

There were still four or five Visitors buzzing the two canoes. None of them seemed to be aware of the hijacking that had just taken place under their noses. John tried to steer the disk, found it easy, and joined the skirmish once again.

Tyler shot another Visitor off his disk just as John came up behind one of the others. Reaching over, he tapped the alien on the shoulder.

The Visitor stopped firing his laser pistol and turned his head slowly. John smiled at him.

"See that?" John pointed into the distance with his index finger.

The Visitor looked away to see what John meant. When he turned around again, he was met with a terrific uppercut that lifted him right off the disk, headfirst into the water.

"All *right*!" Chris shouted from below.

John smiled, but not for long. A Visitor was coming right for him, laser pistol pointed straight at his head.

Something like a thunderclap exploded, and the Visitor clutched his chest as he flew into the water.

Marie sat below in the rocking canoe, shotgun smoking in her hands. The smell of gunpowder permeated the damp air.

The remaining two Visitors glanced at each other and shot off into the swamp as fast as their disks would carry them.

Chapter 25

"These men are not our enemies," John told the assembled tribe in front of the visitors' center. "I saw them fight bravely against the Visitors, and I believe they will help us."

"You saw them fight for their lives, John Tiger," a middle-aged man in the crowd said, "but if they hadn't come here, maybe Martin Wooster would be alive today."

"Martin knew what he was getting himself into," John replied. "I was there when he invited these men into his office to talk. He decided it would be best for our people if he helped them find the Visitors' camp."

"They left us alone until these CIA men came," a woman shouted angrily. "Maybe they'll leave us alone when they're gone."

"Leave us alone?" Marie spoke up. "Do you call kidnapping people whenever they stray away from the village leaving us alone?"

"We don't know that they were kidnapped," the woman persisted. "You want to believe that, Marie, and we all know why. You don't want to believe your man walked out on you."

"Billy didn't walk out on me," Marie said through clenched teeth. "He was taken forcibly."

"How do you know? Did you see it happen?"

"I don't have to see it rain to know there are clouds in the sky," Marie replied.

"I think Marie's right," another woman put in. "Nothing has been right around here lately. The animals are nervous, people are vanishing, and there are strange sounds out in the swamp at night."

A murmur of agreement rose from the crowd.

"Look," John Tiger said, "we're five, six hundred strong. We can put up a fight, at least. The rest of the Visitors were driven from the Earth, but those out in the swamp stayed. That means they've developed a cure for the Red Dust. All of the earth is in danger once again unless they are stopped."

Ham and Chris looked at each other as the Indians shouted their approval of what John had just said. "He's quite a politician," Chris said, grinning.

"The next chief," Ham agreed.

"Let's go out there and deal with them now!" someone shouted.

The crowd roared, some of the men starting toward their homes to get guns.

"Wait a minute!" Ham shouted. "Wait just a minute!"

After a few seconds they calmed down enough for Ham to be heard.

"I know you're ready to fight," he said, "but it's going to require a little planning. You can't just run out there and start shooting."

"Why not?" several people wanted to know.

"Because you'll lose."

An irritated buzz rippled through the crowd.

"You won't lose because of lack of courage or fighting ability. You'll lose because the Visitors have got advanced technology. You just don't have the weapons to fight them with."

"Well, what are we going to do, Ham Tyler?" Marie

demanded. "Wait here until we're all killed? At least we can go down fighting."

"I didn't say you shouldn't fight, only that you don't have the weapons to fight them. I can get you those weapons."

"Do it, then," John Tiger said. "Let's not waste any more time."

"Just lead me to a phone," Ham said. "And I'll have them here by this time tomorrow, if not sooner."

"What do we do in the meantime?"

"Plan our strategy." Ham flashed a rare grin. "We can beat those lizards."

John nodded and led Ham and Chris inside the building to Martin's office. Marie went with them.

"So they've appointed you acting chief," Ham said.

"That's right."

Ham picked up the phone and dialed Los Angeles. In the quiet room, the tone could be heard even over the air conditioner.

After four rings, the receiver clicked. "Hello?" said a faint voice.

"Hello, this is Ham Tyler calling. I'd like to speak to Mike Donovan or Julie Parrish, please."

Chapter 26

"Do you find our laboratories interesting, Dr. Fontaine?" Morrow asked as they walked through the compound's genetic facility.

"I'd be lying if I said no," Sabrina admitted.

They stopped to look at a hologram magnifying a cell to the size of a football. In three dimensions all the organelles could be seen from any angle, even while they were inside the pulsing cell wall. Color enhancement emphasized the difference between the genes that were found naturally inside the cell and those introduced in the laboratory.

"Sit down at the console," Dr. Morrow instructed her. "Get the feel of it."

She touched a red rectangle on the console, and it began to glow. The hologram showed a gene, like a tiny red coil, being inserted into the cell.

"Is this a training device?" she asked.

"No, you have just added a gene to that cell."

"How does it work?" Sabrina asked.

"There is a miniaturized robot that responds positronically

to your command. We can arrange it so that you need only speak to make it do your will."

Make it do your will. That was the key to the way the Visitors thought. Making things do your will—and people too. To Dr. Morrow, a perfect world would be one in which he was never questioned, never challenged—except by his superiors, of course.

"It's an amazing machine, Dr. Morrow," Sabrina said. "What I don't understand is why, when you have technology like this, you need me and Dr. Thorkel."

"There were others too. Like you, they refused to cooperate. After a while I grew tired of their intransigence."

The iciness of his tone chilled her to the marrow, but she tried not to show it. "But that doesn't answer my question, Dr. Morrow."

"Very well, I shall answer you." He bowed his head in thought for a moment and then said, "We wouldn't need you if we had more time."

If they had more time. Perhaps the antitoxin didn't cope with the bacteria for very long. A matter of weeks or months, perhaps.

"Of course," Dr. Morrow continued, "we would require no aid from native scientists otherwise. But there are certain peculiarities about mammalian gene structure that are puzzling. In time we would come to understand them, but . . ."

"But there is no time," Sabrina finished for him. "I see."

"Yes, clever creature that you are, I knew that you would comprehend our situation once your stubbornness was overcome."

"I'm only doing this to save Jack, you know."

"Yes, but I see your scientific curiosity is already piqued by what you've seen here. In time I am certain that you'll wish to work with me without coercion."

Sabrina started to protest, but then she thought better of it. Perhaps it was a better strategy to remain silent and let Morrow labor under his delusion that she wouldn't be able to resist. If she continually voiced her true feelings, she might find herself at an even greater disadvantage.

"Come," Dr. Morrow said. "I want to show you something, Dr. Fontaine."

"Call me Sabrina," she said.

Dr. Morrow seemed pleased. "Sabrina, if you'll follow me."

He led her through a warren of laboratories and storage areas. At the end of a long corridor, two sentries stood in front of a door.

"What do you think our work is here on Earth?" Dr. Morrow asked as they approached the door.

"You've succeeded in developing an antitoxin," Sabrina said, measuring her words carefully, "and you've achieved remarkable results in genetic engineering."

"Yes, we've synthesized a virus that holds the bacteria at bay for a while." He looked straight at her, a cipher behind his dark glasses. "You guessed that, didn't you?"

"Guessed?" She tried to play dumb. "Guessed what?"

"That we have not been completely successful in fighting the Red Dust. But we will be, in the end."

They stood before the two lizard-faced sentries now. Dr. Morrow removed a pointed crystal object from his lab coat pocket.

"The things we have just been discussing are extraneous to our real work. Behold."

He opened the door.

Across the threshold were endless banks of tiny, podlike sacs. Inside them were infants, curled in the fetal position with their eyes shut. They were breathing, floating in nutrient fluid within the artificial wombs. As Sabrina examined them more closely, she saw that the babies had characteristics of both humans and Visitors. Some were pink and some were green, but the pink ones had ridges in their skulls or clawed fingers, while the green ones possessed upturned noses, puckered little mouths, or tufts of red hair on their scaly heads.

It was horrible but fascinating.

"You have heard of the child Elizabeth?" Dr. Morrow asked. "Her birth was an experiment that succeeded. But even so, we don't quite know how it succeeded. You might say it was an accident. We are very close to understanding how it worked. That is our real purpose here."

"And when you understand how it worked?" Sabrina asked. "What then?"

"Then there will be another child like Elizabeth, and we will raise it."

Chapter 27

The two soldiers stood before Dr. Morrow. His human makeup made him no less intimidating in their eyes. They waited for him to speak.

"So you let them escape," he said in their own tongue.

"We were outnumbered," one of them blurted out.

"Then you should have died."

They both fell silent. They had just heard the death sentence, and there was nothing they could do to change it. They exchanged glances, both of them wishing they had never been assigned Earth duty.

A communication device on Dr. Morrow's desk trilled, announcing a visitor outside his quarters. "Go now," he said to the unfortunate soldiers. "I will deal with your execution later."

The door slid open, and they nearly collided with the incoming Dr. Thorkel.

"Dr. Thorkel," Morrow said. "So good of you to come."

As if he had any choice, having been summoned. "What was wrong with those two?" he asked.

"Nothing, nothing. Please come in and sit down."

Dr. Thorkel selected a chair and seated himself, folding his arms over his chest as he waited for Dr. Morrow to tell him what was on his mind. He had come to expect the alien scientist to toy with him a bit before coming to the point.

"You are a Terran," Dr. Morrow began, "and I am a Sirian."

"Yes." Dr. Thorkel could hardly argue with that. "Our ways are very different," he offered, "in some respects."

"Indeed." Dr. Morrow started pacing the floor. "And yet we have succeeded in producing a child who possesses the best of both races."

"The child Elizabeth, known as the star child."

"We are coming very close to duplicating that experiment's results. We have come, in fact, to that point in the proceedings when we must select the proper breeding stock for that purpose."

"Do you have someone in mind?" Dr. Thorkel asked, fearing that he already knew who it would be.

Dr. Morrow stopped pacing. "I thought Dr. Fontaine would do quite nicely."

"She's a healthy human female, it's true," Dr. Thorkel said, "but she might be a bit old for such a physical ordeal."

"Yes, but I'm afraid that the time element points to her as the logical choice."

Dr. Thorkel bowed his head. The poor woman, he thought. He had to bear part of the responsibility for this. Perhaps there was still a chance of talking Morrow out of it.

"Have you given any thought to whom you might select as the—father?" he asked.

"There are technicians here, biologists, soldiers. No one with really outstanding qualities—except for a single individual."

"And that individual—modesty prevents you from saying—is Dr. Morrow himself."

"You see my position, then, Dr. Thorkel. There is really no other possibility."

There was the possibility that Dr. Morrow had rationalized his position, of course, but Dr. Thorkel was in no position to mention that at the moment. Still, he would do what he could to dissuade the alien from his mad scheme. It was the least he could do for Sabrina Fontaine.

"Though I am familiar with many of your planet's customs," Dr. Morrow said, "the mating rituals have an odd intimacy that would require a great deal of study for me to master them. That is why I have asked you to come here today."

"You want me to teach you our . . . mating rituals? I'm afraid I never learned them very well myself."

"I haven't the time nor the inclination to learn them, Dr. Thorkel. I want you to explain my decision to Dr. Fontaine."

Dr. Thorkel nearly fell out of his chair. Morrow wanted him to play John Alden to his Captain Miles Standish. The entire situation was absurd, but he didn't dare laugh at Morrow.

"I'll see what I can do," he said solemnly.

The perfect human mask Dr. Morrow wore brightened. "Thank you," he said, smiling. "I knew you'd understand."

Dr. Thorkel stood, permitting Dr. Morrow to see him to the door. Outside, he waited until he was safely out of the sentries' earshot before he burst into wild laughter. He really couldn't control himself for a few minutes, having to stop and prop himself up against a bulkhead. Tears came to his eyes every time he thought of Morrow's awkward proposition.

And then he thought of what it would mean to Dr. Fontaine. It wasn't so funny after that. Why did Morrow desire her, an alien woman? Many of the Visitors had shown an attraction for humans of both sexes. Very odd. Perhaps it was some racial inferiority complex, or perhaps they were partly mammalian. That might explain how Elizabeth had been conceived.

But this was mere conjecture. He had better go to Sabrina and tell her what Dr. Morrow had in mind.

Chapter 28

"Ham says it's a death camp," Mike Donovan said, "hidden out there in the Everglades."

"I'll be damned," Elias Taylor said. "Those lizards are harder to get rid of than cockroaches."

"And a lot more dangerous," Julie Parrish added.

The three comrades-in-arms strolled through a warehouse in downtown Los Angeles where a cache of alien weapons was stored. The crates full of lasers were the bounty from a hundred small-scale battles and street skirmishes.

"Do you think we should use the L.A. Mother Ship?" Julie asked.

"It would be like swatting a fly with a sledgehammer," Mike said. "We could blast that installation right out of the swamp, but then we'd never know what they were up to—and it might be pretty important."

Julie scratched her head through her blond hair. "How about a skyfighter?"

"We can fly one out to Florida. The Visitors must have at least one, or they wouldn't be there."

"Most likely more than one," Elias said, slamming his hand

down on a crate. "So I say there's nothing wrong with taking the Mother Ship over there and putting them out of operation once and for all."

"What about the people they've taken prisoner, Elias?" Julie reminded him.

"They're probably lunch meat by now," Elias said. "But I guess we can't be sure."

"Right," Mike said. "So we take a shuttle full of weapons to the local people. Ham is helping them organize a resistance. He said he could hardly talk them into waiting for us."

"That's the spirit."

"What do you think they're up to out there, Julie?" Mike asked. "Ham seems to think it's a scientific compound of some kind. Do you concur?"

"I don't know, Mike. It seems likely, though. A covert operation to experiment on humans that was left behind when the Visitors' armada was forced to flee."

"If that's the case, they must expect the Visitors to come back en masse," Elias said. "Most people are starting to think we've seen the last of 'em. Maybe this will wake 'em up."

"Yeah, it might," Mike agreed.

The hologram of Dr. Morrow was slightly larger than life so that he appeared bloated, floating a foot off the floor.

"I've been pleased with how well you are doing with your researches," Medea said, "and now you say the humans have found you out."

"Four of them have escaped our guards," Dr. Morrow said. "From what they told me, the guards believed them to be local swamp dwellers. Hardly any cause for alarm. Those in authority would never take their claims seriously."

"Your reading of human social customs is superficial," Medea snapped. "Their claims may very well be taken seriously."

"Then perhaps a raid on their village would silence them."

"Only if you can be certain you can kill them all."

"If we strike with our full force at night—"

"It might work. I'll have to think about it."

"There isn't much time," Dr. Morrow reminded her.

"There's enough. You say you are on the verge of a great scientific breakthrough," Medea said. "Otherwise, I might dispatch a ship to get you off Earth."

"I see no reason why the experiment cannot be concluded in space, Medea."

"You have found a suitable human female for the control."

"Yes."

"And who will impregnate the woman?"

"I will, Medea."

This was a surprise. "*You?* Are you certain this is wise?"

"There is really no one else here who will do."

"Doctor Morrow, you just said that the experiment can be concluded in space. There are many available males on this ship alone, not to mention the other ships in the fleet. How can you claim to be the only possibility for the insemination?"

"I know the woman," Dr. Morrow said. "I have been working with her."

Was that a touch of panic she heard in his voice? "What of it?" she asked, testing him. "You can still work with her after the insemination, can't you?"

"Yes, but there are human customs and mores to consider."

"Since when do we have to pander to their primitive rituals?" Medea demanded.

"It is best not to have her disturbed during the conception stage," Dr. Morrow insisted desperately. "It seems to work best when the human female is familiar with the inseminator, when a certain intimacy is—"

"Enough, Dr. Morrow," Medea commanded. "You have no idea how obvious you are."

Dr. Morrow was silent for a few moments, and then he said softly, "What do you mean?"

"You are infatuated with the human woman."

"No, I—"

"Yes, I know. You're only interested in her for the good of our war effort and for science."

"Of course."

"Of course," Medea said sarcastically. "You forget that I have tasted the fruits of earthly love, and I know how intoxicating a human can be."

"Then you will assign someone else?" Dr. Morrow asked, clearly disheartened.

"Not at all. You shall have your human lover, Dr. Morrow—whether she likes it or not."

Chapter 29

Sabrina could hardly believe what Dr. Thorkel was saying.

"Are you trying to tell me that . . . that *alien* is in love with me?"

"Something like that, Doctor."

"This is incredible. I simply can't believe what you're telling me."

Thorkel couldn't say what he was thinking because he knew their conversation was being listened to. But perhaps he could hint at it, at least.

"You should be pleased that he has selected you, Dr. Fontaine," he said. "Think of the advantages such an honor will present to you."

Sabrina frowned. Even now, Dr. Thorkel didn't seem to understand the extent of Dr. Morrow's evil madness. He moved closer to her.

"Dr. Fontaine," he said, "you are a credit to scientists everywhere in the universe."

Before she could move away, he embraced her. She began to

struggle, but then he whispered something in her ear that made her stop.

"Use his infatuation to get us out of here," he told her before letting go of her waist. "Lead him on."

She saw the intensity in his eyes as he released her. An instant later he was the same old Milquetoast Dr. Thorkel, prattling about how wonderful her mating with Dr. Morrow would be. She saw the wisdom in what he was doing and understood that he was not a bad man; he had been misled by Dr. Morrow's clever lies in his thirst for knowledge. But now he was on her side, and she had gained a valuable ally.

"When will you receive Dr. Morrow?" he asked.

"Perhaps I've been too hasty," Sabrina said. "The idea is so new to me, you see. I'll have to collect my thoughts for a while."

"Of course," Dr. Thorkel said. "I'll leave you alone now so you can consider the glorious future our friends, the Visitors, have in store for you."

With that he walked out, leaving Sabrina alone in her minute, cell-like apartment. She sat down, realizing that because of what Dr. Thorkel had said, she now had a chance of getting out of the compound. By holding out on Dr. Morrow, stringing him along, she might be able to save Jack. And if she didn't play her cards right, she might be the cause of his death.

Marie had fire in her eyes. "We've got to act soon. We can't wait forever for those people to bring us weapons. Every minute we sit here people could be dying in that death camp."

"I know it's hard, Marie," John Tiger said, "but Tyler is right. We can't go out there and fight them with shotguns and machetes. Our people had to fight invaders who had superior weapons once before, and look what happened. Half of our ancestors ended up marching on the Trail of Tears—and they were the *survivors* of the war against the white man."

"Not everybody marched," Marie said. "Some people stayed in the swamp."

"Hiding like animals from the power of our enemies," John

said. " 'Those who are ignorant of history are doomed to repeat its mistakes.' "

"Where did you get that fancy quote?"

"From Billy, the college man of the family."

Someone knocked on the office door.

"Come in," John said.

"How are you holding up?" Ham said, entering. Chris was right behind, his bulk filling the doorway.

"We're okay," Marie replied. "We were just discussing philosophy."

"Well, there's not much else to do until Donovan gets here with the lasers."

"We'll try to be patient," Marie said, having benefited from John's little lecture.

The phone rang.

"Hello," John said after picking it up. He turned to Ham. "It's for you."

Ham took the receiver and identified himself. The others could hear a man's voice speaking faintly on the line.

"Yeah," Ham said. "Well, isn't there anything you can do?"

The crackling, distant voice said something nobody but Ham could hear.

"Okay, we'll go for it." He hung up.

"What is it?" Marie asked, sensing bad news.

Showing no emotion, Ham said, "The skyfighter they had stocked the weapons with has malfunctioned. There's a Visitor technician working on it, but it's going to take time. In the meantime, they're putting the armaments aboard another sky-fighter."

"So they're coming, then?" John said.

"Yeah, they're coming. But there's going to be a delay."

"But we can't afford a delay," Marie said, frustration tearing at her insides. "People's lives depend on our getting there soon."

"I know," Ham said, "and that's just what we're going to do."

Chapter 30

Jack wondered for the millionth time what they had in store for him. He had expected to be fed to the monster who had killed T.J., but they'd just kept him locked in this little plastic room, feeding him and watching him ever since they had murdered his friend. God, how he burned to avenge T.J. If he ever got out of this cage—*when* he got out of it, he corrected himself. He wasn't going to give up the ghost, not until he had gotten some revenge.

He had one ace in the hole: they had taken the laser pistol away from him during the escape attempt, but not the crystal key.

He didn't know how many doors it would open in the compound, but it had to open some. Of course, he would have to get loose again before he could use it, but as long as he was alive, there was always a chance.

Jack's reverie was disturbed by the whoosh of his cell door opening.

"Feeding time at the zoo?" he said without bothering to turn around.

"Jack . . ."

For a few seconds, he was afraid to look. He had dreamed of hearing that sweet voice for so long now that he was certain he must be asleep. It might have been some horrible trick the Visitors were playing on him, a simulacrum of Sabrina rather than the real thing.

Prepared for any eventuality, he turned around.

Sabrina stood there, the light from the corridor a soft corona around her shapely form.

"Sabrina," he said, "is that really you?"

"Yes, Dr. Morrow has consented to let me see you for a few minutes."

He walked over to her, reached out, and tentatively touched her cheek. It was soft and warm, exactly as he remembered it. How could an illusion be so flawless?

"Have they harmed you in any way?" he asked.

"No, they've treated me rather well, considering."

"I'm sorry you had to see what happened to T.J."

"That man in the arena—God, it was horrible."

"He was my friend." Jack felt tears coming to his eyes in his sorrow and frustration. "He was trying to help me find you when they captured us."

"Oh, Jack." She held him, squeezing his massive body against her. "I'm so sorry."

Jack wanted to make love to her, and he knew she wanted him, but they were being watched. He would never permit Sabrina to suffer such degradation. She clung fiercely to him, though, as if she didn't realize they were in a goldfish bowl.

"Hold me, Jack," she said, nibbling on his neck. "They can't hear us if we whisper like this." And then in a louder voice: "I've missed you so much."

So she did know. "I never thought I'd see you again, baby," he said, kissing her.

"You should be grateful to Dr. Morrow for this," Sabrina said.

Even knowing that she was only acting, he still felt resentment boiling in his guts at the very thought of owing anything to the monster who had imprisoned them and killed T.J. He said nothing, sensing that he would not be very convincing if he went along with Sabrina on this.

"We're going to get out of here," he whispered. "One way or another, we're going to get out."

"Are you certain this will help?" hissed Dr. Morrow. "It seems almost counterproductive to me. If she . . . loves this man, then she is less likely to cooperate in mating with me."

Dr. Thorkel looked up at him. "Trust me," he said, marveling inwardly at his salesmanship. "She will be so thankful to you for what you've done that no favor will be too great for you to ask."

Morrow stopped pacing and looked quizzically at his human assistant. "Is this typical of human behavior?"

"Read our romance novels. Watch soap operas. Read confession magazines."

"I haven't time for all that," Morrow said as if cursing his luck.

I know you haven't, Dr. Thorkel thought, or you'd realize I'm lying. One of the things that was different about humans and Visitors was the human capacity for change and growth. Because Albert Thorkel had cooperated up to now, Dr. Morrow assumed he always would. He couldn't possibly understand how the sight of the man being butchered in the experimental combat area could so drastically alter a man's perspective on the Visitors. Science was the greatest thing in Thorkel's life, but science's greatness was commensurate with its service to mankind. He valued what he had learned from the Visitors, but he loathed the cruel ways they applied their knowledge. They seemed to think human beings were little more than lab animals.

"Trust me," he repeated.

"I suppose I have little choice," Dr. Morrow complained, leaning forward menacingly. "But just to make sure you remain trustworthy, I have something to show you."

"What?" Dr. Thorkel asked.

"You'll see." Morrow gestured for him to follow him out the door. "We'll go for a little walk now."

Doing as he was told, Dr. Thorkel sensed that he was not going to like what he was about to see.

Chapter 31

"How's it going in there, Willie?" Mike Donovan asked, peering into the antigravity core's gleaming shell.

"Lowly," Willie said, "very lowly."

Mike smiled in spite of the tension. "You mean 'slowly,' Willie."

"Yes—slowly. These smaller engines are extremely complex, but I shall have it sicked in a short time."

"Licked."

"Sorry?" Willie's puzzled look amused Mike.

"You said you'll have it 'sicked.' I think you meant 'licked.'"

"Thank you. One day I shall master the intricacies of your language, no doubt, but it will take time."

"Well, we don't have any more time now. You'll have to finish working on the skyfighter engine when we come back from Florida."

"We must go, then?"

"All the armaments have been loaded into one of the other skyfighters. Ham needs us now, but we still have to cross a continent."

"I wanted to accompany Ham and Chris when they left."

"I know, Willie," Mike said, patting him on the shoulder as Willie climbed out of the core, "but he thought this mission would work out best if he and Chris went alone. It looks as if he was right—up to a point."

"And we have reached that point now?"

"Something like that."

They crossed the immense docking bay and entered a sky-fighter around which dozens of people, both human and Visitor, milled. The last few crates were being transferred from the ailing skyfighter at that very moment.

As they boarded, they were greeted by Julie and Elias, who were supervising the loading. Willie checked the command console while the last crates were put in place. There was barely enough room for the four comrades-in-arms to move, the skyfighter was so full.

"It's a good thing we have antigravity engines," Julie joked. "A conventional aircraft would never get off the ground with such a heavy cargo."

"We did bring a few extras," Elias said, "just to add a little spice."

"Let's hope we get there in time to use those extras," Mike said.

Willie flipped a toggle and the engines whined. A moment later they were drifting out of the shuttle bay into the clear California night, the stars twinkling around them.

As soon as they were clear of the Mother Ship, they shot out of sight in an instant.

The faster-than-light transmission ended. The Leader had not only approved of the plan to attack the swamp-dwelling rabble before they became an organized resistance force, he wondered why it had not already been done.

This would not go well on Medea's record. Her only chance for recouping what she had lost through hesitation lay in utterly wiping out very human being who could conceivably be aware of the Visitors' presence in the swamp.

This might not be as difficult as it seemed, she mused. The one authority figure who had stumbled onto the compound was a minor law official who had been liquidated. His companion was in captivity, as was the woman he loved. Sooner or later someone would discover that the village—reservation, they called it—had been destroyed, but by then it would be too late. Anyone else in the vicinity would have little effectiveness against the Visitors, since the reservation, the locus of any organized resistance, would have been destroyed.

Then Dr. Morrow could bring his precious Dr. Sabrina Fontaine aboard a Mother Ship. Medea felt a certain curiosity about her herself. She was a woman who could exercise significant power over an analytical mind like Dr. Morrow's. She must be an interesting woman.

But there was no time for such conjectures now. Word was undoubtedly spreading among the swamp dwellers. Their little revolution had to be nipped in the bud.

Her hand played across the communication console. A moment later, Dr. Morrow's face—wearing his bearded human disguise, as always—hung suspended in front of her.

"The Leader agrees with me that you should attack the swamp dwellers. Make preparations to do so at once," Medea said.

"Excellent, Commander," Dr. Morrow replied.

"You will bring the prototype with you to see how it behaves in actual field conditions."

"Yes."

"And if it proves as efficient in the field as it has in controlled testing, you will immediately begin development of an army of such hybrid fighting creatures."

Dr. Morrow was so pleased he could hardly speak, and he nodded his head vigorously in approval.

"At the same time, you will begin your attempt to impregnate Dr. Sabrina Fontaine. We can fight the puny inventions the humans use to repulse us—it is only a matter of time until we develop an antitoxin with permanent effects, thanks largely to your superb work, Doctor—but we can do

nothing if they harness the potential power of the star child,
Elizabeth."

"I am eager to begin, Commander," Dr. Morrow said, trembling with joyous anticipation.

"I'm sure you are," Medea replied, ending the transmission
as curtly as the Leader had ended their conversation a few
minutes earlier. "Begin at once."

Chapter 32

"We've got to start without the weapons I promised you," Ham told the Indians and swamp rats as they stood in the saw grass at dawn. "They'll be here soon, but we just can't wait any longer."

"You said we couldn't fight 'em without those lasers," a grizzled, gray-bearded swamp rat said. "How come you changed your mind?"

"I haven't," Ham admitted. "But we can surprise them. I've given Mike Donovan a pretty good idea of where we'll be, and there are sensors aboard the skyfighter that will lead them to the death camp once they're in close proximity."

"What good's that gonna do us if we're all killed?"

"The infantry in World War Two used to say, 'They can kill you but they can't eat you.' In this case, they'll do both. So if that scares you so much you can't fight, we don't want you with us."

The bearded man hung his head in shame as Ham went on: "All we can do is hold our own until reinforcements arrive with the weapons. I know Mike Donovan, and I'm certain he'll be there. There's nothing more I can say to convince you. If you don't think we've got a chance, you can stay behind. But once we've started, I'll personally shoot anyone, man or woman, who tries to turn back. This is no game."

There followed some murmuring, a few angry glances at Graybeard, and shouts of "We're with you!"

"Let's go," Ham said.

Hundreds of people dissipated like swamp fog, slipping between the trees and cycads as elusively as tendrils of early morning mist.

"He's getting impatient, Sabrina," Dr. Thorkel whispered as he picked up a drinking tube from the plastic table.

Then, in a booming voice, he said, "Dr. Morrow wanted me to tell you how well our work is going and to ask you to meet with him today."

"Meet with him? Where?"

Dr. Throkel frowned. "In his quarters or yours, as you prefer."

Sabrina said nothing.

"He showed me something that frightened me," Dr. Thorkel whispered. He had intended to keep it to himself, but he couldn't. It was too horrible. Besides, it was a further incentive for Sabrina to string Dr. Morrow along. He saw the revulsion and fear in her eyes, but only for a moment.

"About Dr. Morrow's suggestion . . ." he began.

Sabrina tried not to look rueful. She had to think fast, or they would be back to zero. "But, uh, the proxy phase of courtship isn't over yet," she said. "In fact, it's hardly begun."

"Yes, I know. I'll explain that to him, but I don't know if he'll . . . understand the depth of your commitment to . . . traditional mating rituals."

Sabrina nodded. They had to put off Dr. Morrow just a little longer, until the three of them had a chance at freedom. Maybe her best bet was to see Dr. Morrow herself, to make some excuse that would keep him at arm's length a little longer. The proxy bit didn't seem to be working very well anymore, so she had to come up with something completely different.

"Very well, I'll see him later today," she said, "if he isn't too busy."

"I'm sure he'll find time," Dr. Thorkel said, rising to kiss her on the cheek and whispering, "unfortunately."

He set down his drink and left Sabrina, gazing sadly back at her as the door closed. He had done his best, but it apparently wasn't good enough; it seemed that his efforts had come too late to be of much use. Disheartened, he returned to his rooms.

Sabrina was racking her brain for something to stall Dr. Morrow with a little longer. Good God, she couldn't let him touch her, even to save her own skin. But it wasn't her skin she was trying to save, she reminded herself. It was Jack's.

Jack. . . . As far as Morrow knew, Jack was the only man she'd ever known intimately. Maybe she could play on that—and Morrow's ignorance of human customs—to not only put the alien off but to get Jack out of his cell too.

"Necessity is the mother of invention," she muttered, "and what a mother this invention promises to be."

The two sentries, nameless like all Sirians bred for military service, didn't want to die. They had been assigned no duty since their fateful meeting with Dr. Morrow and now awaited the final dispatch which would inform them of the method of their deaths. Their quarters had become a prison cell.

"Do you think they'll feed us to that creature," one of them said, "the way they disposed of the human?"

"I don't know," the other replied. "Does it matter?"

"No, I suppose not." His companion did little but brood over their situation while the first condemned sentry desired a little conversation to enliven his last hours.

"I suppose they'll be better off when we're gone," the second sentry said. "And they'll destroy any genes that might produce others like us, to weed out undesirable elements from the military."

A mosquito buzzed in the tiny room. The first sentry's tongue lashed out and snapped it out of the air. He swallowed the tidbit before speaking again. "It doesn't seem right."

"Right? What does right have to do with it? We've committed an unpardonable crime, and we're being condemned to death. That's all there—"

The door slid open, and Dr. Morrow himself entered. The two sentries fell silent, their argument forgotten.

"I have arrived at the method of your execution," he said. They waited.

"You will die in the experimental combat area," Dr. Morrow informed them coolly.

"No," sentry number one said. "You're not going to make us face that terrible beast."

"Quite the contrary." His human mask was inscrutable. "What I have in mind should be even more amusing."

"What, then?" the second sentry asked wearily.

"You will face one another in the arena."

The two sentries looked at each other as Dr. Morrow emitted a sound unnervingly like human laughter and made his exit.

Chapter 33

Dr. Morrow had enjoyed telling the two sentries the absurd nature of their demise before seeing Sabrina. The day was going very well, indeed. Her decision to at last receive him had been inspirational. Those two cowering salamanders would provide the entertainment at the celebration before he inseminated her.

He walked purposefully toward her apartment. This was to be a great moment in the history of science—not to mention the history of his people.

For a while he had been afraid he would have to use force, but the presence of the human, Jack Stern, in the compound had convinced her to be accommodating. And now, through the intervention of Dr. Thorkel, she was warming to him as though he were a member of her own race.

He was at her door now. Inserting his key, he waited for it to open and entered.

"Dr. Morrow," Sabrina said, smiling at him. "Won't you please come in?"

"Yes." The door closed behind him. "Thank you."

She smiled again. Strange how these creatures showed their

fangs, even beneath their human-disguised teeth, when they were happy.

"Can I offer you something?"

"Just . . . water," he said. It wouldn't do to eat a rodent in front of her. Of course she didn't have any rodents anyway.

She poured ice water into a drinking tube and set it on the table. "Won't you sit down?" she asked.

He sat down.

"I think I'll have a little wine," she said. "I hope you don't mind."

"No, of course I don't," he stammered. "Please help yourself."

As she filled her wineglass, Dr. Morrow thought how much this was like something on television. He had witnessed such scenes many times in his training, but experiencing it was quite something else again. Though his heart was fibrillating, he was enjoying it enormously.

"You know," Sabrina said, "you're a very attractive man."

Dr. Morrow swelled with the compliment, but her words confused him as much as they pleased him. She had called him a man, but surely she knew what his physical appearance really was. She had seen many Sirians in the compound; she was doubtless aware of his makeup, perfect as it was. Perhaps she had seen him as he really was beneath the cosmetic veneer.

"Dr. Thorkel has spoken to you about"—Morrow found it such an embarrassing, awkward word—"the lovemaking?"

"Yes, he has." She leaned forward, exposing her cleavage. For the first time, Dr. Morrow noticed how formfitting and elegant her free-flowing garment was. It seemed to add to her allure.

"There is a myth among my people," Sabrina said, "about a beautiful garden and the first two people in the world. They are innocent until a snake visits them and introduces them to sin. I find that idea very erotic."

"Ah—fascinating." This explained much. Dr. Morrow warmed to the subject of mythology. "We have a myth too."

"Oh?"

"Yes. It concerns my people at the beginning of time. A race of apelike creatures ruled our world then, subjugating our ancestors and stirring resentment and a desire for vengeance in their hearts."

Sabrina stared at him strangely. Was that understanding in her eyes, or was it a sudden contempt brought upon her by his description of the myth? They were so complex, these mammalian creatures, so driven by primitive desires and superstition. If only she would say something so he would know how she felt.

"That's a wonderful story," she said, "but let's talk about us."

"About—courtship, you mean?"

"Uh-hunh, and about more than that."

Dr. Morrow was so excited he could hardly contain himself.

"We've come to the end of the proxy stage now," she said. "About to enter the crucial phase."

"Crucial phase?" Dr. Morrow asked. This was indeed intricate. "Please explain."

"You must introduce the physical proxy next," Sabrina whispered seductively, leaning closer to him.

"The . . . physical proxy?" What *was* she talking about?

"You don't know about that? Oh, Dr. Morrow, you're so negligent in your study of human folkways."

"I have been preoccupied with other things, I admit."

"Didn't they tell you in your training that a woman can only be introduced to a new partner through her former lover?"

"What? I mean, no, they never told me."

"It will be a beautful experience for the three of us," Sabrina sighed.

"The . . . three of us?"

"Of course." She smiled charmingly. "You, me—and Jack."

For a moment Dr. Morrow couldn't believe his earholes. At length he spoke: "Jack. . . ."

"Of course." She nodded. "You don't think I can just go from one man to the next without the intermediate stage, do you?"

"I suppose not." Anything to complete the experiment successfully.

"Wonderful!" Sabrina said rapturously, clinking her wineglass against Dr. Morrow's drinking tube. "Here's to us!"

Chapter 34

"There it is," Ham said.

"Yes, sir." Chris softly spread two ferns to get a better look. "Look at those holograms. No wonder nobody ever spotted it from the air."

They retreated, walking back to join the others. As they talked, Ham attempted to shape a strategy.

"I think it's a good idea to wait until dark," he said, "even though the lizards see better at night."

"Well, we've got flares. They'll be blinded when we start setting those babies off."

"They'll never expect it tonight, but they know the word is out on them. I wouldn't be surprised if they were planning an attack on their own."

"Makes sense," Chris agreed.

"Let's just hope they don't know you and I are in the neighborhood, partner."

"I don't see how they could, unless they've got a spy on the reservation."

"None of the missing persons have showed up using their left hands, so it looks like we're safe on that count," Ham said.

Chris chuckled as they started around the perimeter. Shielded by thick growth so that little sound escaped, their people had set up camp a mile from the alien compound. There they were cutting down trees, stripping them, and nailing branches across them for handholds and footholds. With these, they would storm the walls, hoping to get enough manpower on the other side to open the gates.

"Gonna be a real old-fashioned siege," Ham said. "Let's just hope the cavalry gets here on time."

Chris and Ham patrolled the perimeter themselves for three reasons: they were both crack shots, they were the only ones who had laser pistols, and they had fought the Visitors before.

So far they hadn't seen any Visitors, or any sign that they'd been seen themselves, but there were still several hours until nightfall.

"Come on, Donovan," Ham said, looking up at the bright sky. "Come *on*."

They were somewhere over Texas when Mike Donovan said, "Willie, can't you push this thing any faster?"

"No," Willie said. "If you want to travel at high speed, you must use the Mother Ship itself. Skyfighters are addended for intraplanetary travel only, and are limited."

"Intended," Mike said, punching a crate.

"Sorry?"

"Intended. You said 'addended,' and I think you meant 'intended.'"

"Thank you, Mike."

"Why didn't we take the Mother Ship?" Elias asked. "We'd be in Florida by now."

"Couldn't risk it," Julie explained. "Something as large as the Mother Ship would be tracked by the Visitors. When they saw the speed it was traveling, they'd know exactly what it was and what it was there for. This way, we can sneak up on 'em."

"If we can find them," Mike added, "and if we get there on time."

He gazed at the viewscreen and saw the Texas plains rushing by. At any other time, he would have thought they were traveling at an exhilarating speed. Today, it seemed as if they were moving as slowly as death itself.

"You will come with us," the sentry's hissing voice commanded.

Jack thought about jumping him, but the laser pistol was trained right at his chest. He wouldn't have a chance. This was it, then. He had no choice but to do as he was told.

Starting out of the cell, he wondered what had become of Sabrina. Dr. Morrow must have finally realized he'd been had. Would he punish her, or would he try to force himself on her?

Would he do worse than that?

There were two more sentries in the corridor, so he had no chance of getting away now. Three lasers was too much to contend with, especially since the sentries were being extremely cautious.

They pushed him roughly toward the middle of the compound. In a few moments, they stood before a door. One of the sentries produced a crystal key and inserted it in a slot next to the door.

The door opened.

Inside was a dimly lit room. Candelit, in fact. Jack squinted, trying to see what was in store for him. There was a white-jacketed, bearded, silver-haired figure sitting in a chair. Dr. Morrow.

Sitting across the table from Morrow was a woman, sipping from a wineglass, dressed in a flimsy nightgown.

It was Sabrina.

"Leave us," Dr. Morrow commanded the sentries.

They did as they were told. As soon as the three of them were alone, Sabrina spoke.

"Hello, Jack," she said.

"Sabrina—what's this all about?" Jack asked, uncertain of what to do.

"We're going to make love, Jack," Sabrina said, as if she were telling him what they were having for dinner.

"What do you mean, 'we'?" Jack asked.

"You and me—and Dr. Morrow."

Chapter 35

"Surely you understand, dear," Sabrina said. "You and I will start, and Dr. Morrow will take over, as is the custom."

The custom? What was she talking about? Had they done something to her mind? Conversion? Or was she bluffing, playing for time with a new tack?

If the latter was the case, he didn't want to blow it.

"Yes, of course," he said.

"Would you care for some wine, Mr. Stern?" Dr. Morrow asked politely. "I understand that is the custom in these matters."

"Yes, I think I will have a glass, thank you."

"I brought these two wineglasses in my suitcase," Sabrina said. "And a bottle of Rothschild '79." She poured him a sparkling glass of wine.

Jack accepted the glass and downed the liquid in a single gulp. It warmed his insides and seemed to help him think a little more clearly while Sabrina acted out her charade. He had no idea what she had told Morrow about human customs.

His best bet was to keep his mouth shut and let her do the talking.

"First, Jack will show you how to kiss me," Sabrina said. "Come here, Jack."

He set down the glass and went around the table. Bending, he kissed Sabrina deeply.

"Any time you feel like it," she whispered in his ear as she nuzzled him, "let him have it."

"Do we go to the bed now?" Dr. Morrow asked.

"Don't be so eager," Sabrina said. "Proper lovemaking requires time and patience. As a scientist, you understand those two virtues, I'm sure."

Jack stood behind Sabrina's chair, caressing her shoulders and kissing her soft neck. God, how he had missed her. But he couldn't involve his feelings now.

"Would you like to try it, Dr. Morrow?" Sabrina asked.

"Try what he has been doing, you mean?" Morrow said eagerly. "Yes, I would."

"Come, then," Sabrina said, beckoning him to join them.

Dr. Morrow pushed back his chair noisily and placed himself next to Jack.

"You saw what he did, Doctor," she said. "Just do the same thing."

Sabrina felt his hands on her neck, indistinguishable from the touch of a human being. And yet he wasn't human. He only wore a human disguise, and he hated humans, as did many of his people, perhaps because of their ancient creation myth.

"That feels good," she said.

Dr. Morrow rubbed her shoulders more vigorously, forgetting Jack's presence. "And now the kiss?" he asked, bending to plant one.

Jack's arm shot out and clamped Morrow's throat in a stranglehold. Morrow gasped as Jack squeezed tighter and tighter.

Sabrina jumped up from the table, shouting as the sentries poured into the room. "He's dead if you don't stay right where you are."

The sentries hesitated.

"You fools," Dr. Morrow choked, "kill them."

Jack put on enough pressure to crush a man's windpipe.

Unable to breathe, Dr. Morrow writhed helplessly in Stern's powerful arms.

"Shoot at us," Jack said, "and I'll tear his head off."

A bit of an exaggeration, Jack knew, but he assumed they knew little of the limits of human strength. They could see that Dr. Morrow was in great pain, and that seemed to be enough.

"Back off," Jack commanded the sentries.

They backed off, moving toward the door. Relieved, Jack relaxed his grip a bit. "Get their guns, Sabrina," he said.

Sabrina started forward when Jack suddenly felt a rending pain in the fleshy part of his forearm.

Dr. Morrow was biting him, his razor-sharp teeth tearing through the human mask he wore. Jack tried to hold on, but the pain was too searingly intense. Dr. Morrow broke free of his grasp.

But before Morrow could get completely away, Jack had him by the hair. A human would have been yanked backward, but not Dr. Morrow. Instead, his scalp tore open, revealing the scaly green hide underneath the pale, synthetic human skin.

Dr. Morrow stepped away, leaving Jack holding the scalp in his hands. Standing between two sentries, Morrow peeled the rest of his mask away.

"There's the thing that wanted to make love to you," Jack said, disgusted.

Dr. Morrow's yellow eyes flashed.

"You'll pay for this!" he screamed. "Both of you!"

Sabrina stood next to Jack, her arm encircling his.

"How touching you both look," Morrow said, regaining some of his composure. "Together again at last."

"You can destroy us, Dr. Morrow," Jack said. "But you can't destroy what we feel for one another."

"Then you will have a chance to demonstrate that feeling, Mr. Stern," Morrow hissed. "Take them to the experimental combat area."

Jack's heart froze. "No, don't take Sabrina there. She didn't know what I was going to do. Take me, but not her."

"Silence!" Morrow shrieked. He turned to his sentries. "To the arena!"

Chapter 36

The two condemned sentries were rudely awakened by boots jostling them from their dreams. Odd dreams of freedom in the case of sentry number one, and in the case of sentry number two, a nightmare of death. The details of their respective dreams faded into vagaries, nothing more than moods, as they were roughly pulled to their feet and marched out into the compound.

"Where are you taking us?" sentry number one demanded.

"They're taking us to our deaths," number two said when none of the guards deigned to answer.

Number one fell silent as they were dragged down a passageway and through a door into the experimental combat area. The place was writhing with spectators seated all the way up to the top of the walls on every side. They hissed and bellowed for blood—his blood, he reflected, and the blood of his moribund friend.

In his special box, centered underneath the far wall, sat Dr. Morrow. The guards pushed the two doomed sentries toward him. Bright lights nearly blinded them.

Dr. Morrow, no longer in his human disguise and wearing a

crimson jumpsuit, lifted his right claw. The throng immediately fell silent.

"I have decided to treat you to an unprecedented spectacle tonight," he boomed, his rasping voice echoing through the suddenly still arena. "But first, a small amusement."

A murmur arose from the crowd at the promise of entertainment.

"These two cowards before you, who ran away from combat with humans, will now have the opportunity to redeem themselves. They will be given primitive weapons and will fight to the death."

The crowd roared its approval.

Dr. Morrow gestured for silence once again. "And the winner will be sent back to the home world in disgrace, to lead a life of drudgery and ostracism."

Hooting and hissing, the crowd showed its eagerness for the spectacle to begin.

The lights shining on the two combatants were dimmed to a level not much brighter than moonlight. As soon as their eyes recovered and adjusted to the more suitable lighting, a guard appeared, carrying long blades with serrated edges.

These were handed to the gladiators. Both of them stood hefting the heavy blades up from the dirt, the crowd noisily exhorting them to begin the fight.

A blue laser beam nearly burned a toe off sentry number two's foot. He lurched forward but still didn't lift the blade.

Another shot made number one jump.

"If you do not try to kill each other," Dr. Morrow assured them from the stands, "I will instruct my guards to slaughter you, make no mistake about that."

"We must try to fight," sentry number one said, "so that at least one of us may live."

The idea of killing his friend was dreadful, but number two had to agree. They had both been created in the same laboratory and shared a common bond. Now they owed it to each other to finish this bloody business as quickly as possible.

They began to warily circle one another, round and round, looking for an opening. To each, it was as if he were reliving his nightmare. One of them saw the chance to live, the other saw nothing but death.

Sentry number one swung his blade. It whistled through the air, missing his opponent by several inches. Many in the crowd shouted encouragement while a few clucked at the obviously half-hearted lunge.

Sentry number two swung wide in response, and the crowd responded with a little more enthusiasm, though there was dissatisfaction in their cries at the feebleness of the combatants' efforts thus far.

They continued to circle one another and occasionally sliced the air with their blades as the crowd grew ever more restless. Dr. Morrow instructed a guard to fire a laser at their feet again, to enliven things.

"If one of you doesn't die here, then you will both die the slowest, most agonizing deaths imaginable."

The energy beams burning their soles, the two friends knew that they had to fight as if they meant it.

Suddenly number one saw the flash of his opponent's blade and felt the fiery pain of a cut on his shoulder.

He raised a claw to the wound, feeling green ichor bubbling out. Shocked and enraged, he charged at his friend without thinking of the consequences. His blade held out to the side, he realized abruptly that he was a vulnerable target. His opponent could have cut him down with a single slice.

Curiously, sentry number two did no such thing. Instead, he lifted his blade high over his head and hesitated, holding his arm up and providing his friend with a clear, unshielded shot at his torso.

Closing the membrane over his eyes in grief, number one cut him down with a single slice.

The crowd raged, its taste for blood thoroughly awakened by this gratuitous killing. The lone sentry, standing over his friend's corpse, wished that he could turn the blade on every one of them.

His friend had let him kill him, fulfilling the dream of each.

Sadly, he allowed the guards to lead him out of the arena so that the next spectacle could be made ready.

Chapter 37

"Leave the dead one there," Dr. Morrow commanded. "And bring out the actors in our next little drama."

The door on the far side of the arena slowly lifted, and two humans were pushed forward: Jack and Sabrina.

Fully half a dozen armed guards followed Jack, their lasers trained on him at every moment. They forced him and Sabrina to the center of the arena, where they stood and waited for . . .

Jack heard a crunching sound at his feet, followed by the unmistakable sound of shifting dirt. He saw a hole open in the arena floor, and a thick column began to rise into the humid night air.

Dr. Morrow shouted a command in the Visitors' tongue, and the guards pulled Sabrina away from Jack. She was taken to the post and bound to it with crimson cords.

"Jack," she whimpered. "What are they doing to me?"

He wanted to go to her, but four weapons were pointed at him. He stood and watched two of the guards finish tying her, wishing that he could get his hands on them for just a few seconds. He swore to himself that if Dr. Morrow came down from his box, he would tear the sadist to bits with his bare hands, lasers or no lasers.

As soon as Sabrina was securely bound, the guards stepped away from her and joined those pointing weapons at Jack.

A hush fell over the crowd as Dr. Morrow addressed them.

"My faithful friends," he said. "You have worked long and faithfully in the service of our cause. Tomorrow, we will launch an attack on the local humans, destroying them all so that no rumor of our presence here can reach their disorganized authorities.

"But tonight, as a prelude to the pleasure that awaits us in the morning, we shall enjoy a spectacle that no one has ever witnessed before. The mating of human woman, man, and—"

Dr. Morrow flung a claw out in the direction of the opposing wall, and a door began to rise from the ground up. Jack watched, his hopes fading as the taloned feet of the prototype came into view, followed by its scaly, tree-trunk-size legs, its armored belly and chest, and finally its hideous fanged snout.

"If Mr. Stern should be so cruel as to kill the poor beast," Dr. Morrow said, "then he and Dr. Fontaine will be set free. But if the beast should kill him . . ."

He left the sentence purposely unfinished. The crowd, at first waiting for him to complete it, slowly began to get the joke. They registered their approbation as loudly as a tidal wave.

So, Jack thought, if Dr. Morrow couldn't have ménage à trois, he would have his revenge with this grotesque travesty of the act he had believed he would perform with Sabrina. But in Dr. Morrow's place would be the prototype, and there would be no mercy.

The gigantic reptile-man emerged from the shadows, slowly at first. Its huge form didn't look as if it could move quickly, but Jack had seen what it could do. No human ever moved that fast.

He would have to outsmart it, if he and Sabrina were to have any chance at all. Never taking his eyes off the advancing monster, he made his way toward the nearest wall.

The reptile-man stopped moving, beady black eyes swiveling from Jack to Sabrina and back again.

"Hey, you!" Jack shouted at it.

The monster turned its immense head toward him.

"That's right," Jack bellowed belligerently. "I'm talking to you, you ugly bastard."

The crowd was stilled at this unexpected behavior. They sensed that they were going to get a better fight than they had bargained for.

The prototype seemed confused at Jack's baiting. After a few seconds, it decided the noise was meaningless and turned back toward Sabrina, who squirmed on the pole tantalizingly.

Seeing that he was losing its attention, Jack looked around him desperately. He picked up a clod of dried mud and hurled it at the monster.

The clod bounced off its armored head. It was only the merest annoyance, Jack was sure, but it was enough to distract the thing from Sabrina, at least for the moment.

"Sabrina," he shouted, "stay still. It's attracted by your movements."

Sabrina was frightened out of her wits, whimpering and struggling to free herself. Nevertheless, she tried to do as Jack said. Taking a deep breath, she relaxed every muscle in her body with a tremendous exertion of will.

"Come on, big boy," Jack yelled, "over here!" He jumped up and down, waving his arms. "What are you, chicken?"

The reptile-man stood squarely facing him, tail lashing angrily. Its misshapen head reared back, and it let out a bone-chilling, subhuman wail.

Jack put his back to the wall. "Come on, you ugly sucker!"

The monster charged.

Chapter 38

Jack spun, scraping one arm against the wall as he came up between the monster's legs in a crouch.

The beast-man smashed headfirst into the wall. There was a resounding *crack!* Staggering, the monster tried to find Jack's remains on the ground, and then realized that it had been outsmarted.

"Very good!" Dr. Morrow shouted from his box. "Very clever indeed, Mr. Stern. But you have only served to enrage the creature further."

Jack tried not to listen. He danced in front of the snarling monster, taunting it, challenging it to come after him again.

"You have already seen its strength," Morrow called to him, "and you know it is impervious to projectile weapons."

The monster's tail snapped like a whip as Jack moved back and forth in front of it.

"But you don't know that we intend to create an army of these warrior beast-men. Imagine them coming out of the swamps, killing and terrorizing humankind, demoralizing you from below while our ships attack you from above." Dr.

Morrow's foot-long tongue shot out of his mouth in delight as he thought of how sweet his vengeance would be.

Opening its cavernous jaws, the monster roared its terrifying subhuman war cry and lunged toward Jack again. Jack stood his ground, watching the monster loom large.

"Jack!" Sabrina screamed, unable to stand it any longer. "Look out!"

The monster's shadow covered him before he acted. Then he threw himself forward on his side and rolled in the dirt. He heard the monster hiss as it tried to stop its forward momentum.

But it was too late. Jack's cross-body block knocked it off balance. The clawed feet tore Jack's shoulder, and he feared that the monster's huge bulk would topple onto him and crush him to death.

Jack kept his body rolling in spite of the agony of his injured shoulder. The monster's tail struck the side of his head, stunning him. He ended up lying flat on his back in the dust, clutching his shoulder. Blinking into the arena lights, he waited for the monster to fall. He had completely lost his bearings in the few seconds since he had jumped in front of the charging beast. He was certain it was going to fall on him and kill him now.

A collision shook the earth. Deliriously, Jack wondered what could have caused it. An earthquake? No, not in this part of the world.

He rose painfully to his knees and saw the flailing monster on its back. It had spun around like a bowling pin and was now as helpless as a newborn babe.

Jack held his shoulder, feeling the warm blood run between his fingers, as he backed away from the fallen behemoth.

He dimly became aware of the screeching crowd. Looking up, he saw a glum Dr. Morrow glaring back down at him.

"You'll have to do better than that," Jack shouted up at him, "if you want to defeat the human race."

Dr. Morrow scowled and gestured for his guard to help his brainchild to its unsteady feet. Four of them jumped into the arena and ran to its aid. As they attempted to help it up, the monster flung its limbs out furiously, and the four guards were sent tumbling into the dust.

Again the crowd roared its delight at the spectacle.

The monster flipped itself over and stood, its saurian head thrown back to emit another roar. This time it circled warily, as it saw Jack doing. It would not be taken by surprise a second time. The strangely human cast of its reptilian features seemed to size up its opponent.

If only he had a gun, Jack thought, but then he remembered with a chill what had happened to T.J. His only chance was to wear it down, outsmart it, but he didn't know how long he could manage that.

The monster suddenly ran straight toward him, each of its heavy footfalls kicking up miniature dust storms, its tail coiling like a cobra about to strike.

With a sinking feeling, Jack saw that it was moving in on him very close to the ground. It wouldn't be tripped this time.

It was almost upon him. Jack took three quick steps and jumped as high as he could, coming down hard right on the monster's back, just above the spot where the spine joined the tail.

The monster howled in pain and frustration. Jack kicked off and landed, squatting two yards behind it.

The crowd could hardly believe its eyes. The spectators screeched and hooted and hissed. The melee seemed to confuse the monster even more.

Jack was beginning to gain more confidence. He reasoned that the prototype, though it had great physical potential, was still inexperienced. It was, after all, only a few days old. Its first opponent had fallen to its gnashing jaws, and it had expected no trouble from Jack. If he could keep it guessing, he could win.

Suddenly the tail lashed out quick as a bullwhip. Before Jack could get out of its way, it coiled around his neck. Like a roped steer, he was pulled toward the monster.

Jerked forward by the monster's tremendous strength, Jack could not resist. He was dragged closer and closer to the slavering jaws.

A scaly, taloned green hand—quite human in the articulation of its joints—reached out for him. He felt the razor-sharp claws sink into the soft flesh of his throat as he was lifted completely off the ground.

The screaming of the crowd was replaced by a ringing as the circulation to his head was cut off. Beyond the arena's lights, he glimpsed the stars, but these were obscured by bright, twinkling motes as he began to lose consciousness.

But before he passed out, he saw the enormous, yawning jaws of the monster opening, engulfing his entire head. It was going to decapitate him with a single bite.

Jack tried to fight, but he couldn't lift his arms. His efforts at kicking resulted in nothing more than spasmodic jerks of his legs. The creature's fetid breath invaded his nostrils.

He was going to die. But what would happen to Sabrina now if he died?

Jack heard a terrible rattling noise and knew it was coming from inside his throat. His windpipe was about to be crushed, while his brain was being deprived of precious oxygen.

The monster's jaws opened even wider, hesitating just for a moment in satisfaction as Jack twisted in the air, dying.

Blue light brilliantly illuminated the monster's hideous, half-human face, blinding it and burning a hole in its armor-plated breast.

Coughing and sputtering, Jack was dropped into the dust as the monster wailed in agony. Jack somehow managed to gain his feet, stumbling to Sabrina as blue laser fire crisscrossed the darkness and hundreds of darkly clad figures streamed over the walls.

Chapter 39

As he came over the top of the wall on the makeshift ladder, John Tiger saw what had so preoccupied the sentries that Ham and Chris had been able to pick them off so easily.

A woman was tied to a thick column in the middle of an open area, a man was staggering to help her, and some *thing* was howling in pain just below the curving rows of seats.

The noises coming out of the thing's jaws stopped John's heart. Horribly distorted though it might have been, it cried out in Billy's voice.

That thing down there—could that have been what they did to his brother?

Holding a .357 Magnum in his hand, John made his way down through the stands, ignoring the tumult around him. Panicking technicians opened a wide swath around him, and he saw a cadre of guards surround a Visitor sitting in a box and hustle him away from the arena through an exit behind his seat.

John came to the lowest row of seats and jumped over the wall into the arena.

The thing was turned away from him, focusing its attention on the woman, whom the injured man was now untying. But

144

when it heard the sound of John dropping into the arena, it spun to face him.

It was a monster, part reptile and part human. The reptile part was bad enough, but the human part bore a strange resemblance to Billy, just as John had feared when he caught his first glimpse of it.

Now the monster stood appraising him, its black eyes somehow the eyes of his brother, its movements a grotesque parody of Billy's.

"What have they done to you?" John said. "What in the name of God have they done to you?"

The thing didn't speak. John realized that it probably couldn't, but he spoke to it again, regardless of the silence his words met.

"Billy, do you know me?" he asked. "I'm your brother, John."

The monster cocked its head uncertainly. Did it understand what he was saying to it?

"Tiger!" a voice rose over the shouting and the gunshots. "Get away from it!"

John was vaguely aware of the voice as Ham Tyler's, but he paid it no heed. He stepped closer to the nightmare thing that was so like his brother.

"You're my brother, Billy," John said. "My brother."

He was within two paces of the thing now. He stopped, hearing a low rumble. Was it some alien machine? No, it was an organic sound, and it came from the throat of the thing he faced.

"It's not your brother!" a woman's voice cried. "They made it from some of his genetic material, but it's not him."

The rumbling grew louder. What was the woman saying? That it wasn't Billy? John couldn't believe that, not while he looked into those eyes. This was his brother, whom John had brought up himself when their parents died. How could he not know the kid when he'd brought him up himself?

The thing that looked like Billy snarled, its tail flexed behind it like a question mark and then straightened. It charged straight at John.

At that moment John realized that this creature, if it had ever been Billy, was somthing else now. He knew he should raise his revolver and fire at it, but it even ran like his brother.

"Shoot!" Jack Stern shouted. "Shoot for the eyes! It's the only chance you've got!"

He couldn't do it. He just couldn't kill this thing, whatever it was. It was too much like Billy. He could only stand and wait for it to pound him into the ground like a tent peg.

A flash of blinding blue light, and the Billy thing wailed in pain as it went down, its legs cut out from underneath it by a laser.

It came toward John like a felled cypress, its scaly arms extended.

One claw on either side of him, John looked into the angry, frightened face of the Billy thing. He was so close he could smell its fetid breath as it thudded into the dust on its chin. Another laser burst hit its misshapen skull.

The thing's body quaked spasmodically for a few seconds, and then it groaned and was still.

John stood staring at the Billy thing's corpse until a Visitor fell from the wall and landed dead a few feet away. He looked up and saw the bearded old swamp rat trying to load his rifle, a Visitor pointing a laser at him, about to fire.

John leveled his revolver at the alien and pumped all six rounds into his chest. As it gasped and writhed its last, the old man looked down at him and held up his thumb in salute.

Jack had finally loosened the taut red cords binding Sabrina. With only one hand, it hadn't been easy, but he had managed. Thank God Ham had been there to lase the reptile-man. He pulled the last cord loose and hugged Sabrina to his chest.

Ham and Chris were firing at a group of sentries on the far wall. The sentries were shooting back, the darkness accentuating their blue laser beams. People were falling all around the two CIA men.

"Come on," Ham yelled at Jack and Sabrina.

Sabrina was having trouble holding Jack up. He was very

weak and unsteady. John Tiger went to their aid, and the two of them managed to get him to the nearest wall.

"Johnny!"

He looked up to see Marie sling a rifle over her shoulder and jump into the arena. She ran to join them.

"You should have stayed up there," John castigated her. "Look at that."

He pointed at the entrances in the stands, from which dozens of armed Visitor guards and sentries emerged. The laser fire was so thick now that it resembled a solid wall of blue light. Ham and the others were falling back, starting to climb over the wall to leave the compound, the tractor beam pushing at them.

"We're cornered," John said. "But why aren't they shooting at us?"

"They probably intend to capture us once the others have been driven back," Sabrina said. "There's no hurry about us— we're stuck here."

"Maybe not," Jack said. He reached into his pocket and withdrew the crystal key. They helped him to the door behind them, and he inserted it in a slot in the wall next to it.

The door slid open.

The four of them rushed through it into the darkness beyond. They tried to help Jack, but he brushed off their hands.

"I'm okay," he said. "Now, let's find our way out of this slaughterhouse."

Guns at the ready, they ran down a long corridor. They came to its end and turned the corner to see twenty armed Visitors charging straight at them.

Chapter 40

"I'll dispatch a Mother Ship immediately," Medea said. "How long do you think you can hold them off?"

"We could hold this rabble off forever," replied Dr. Morrow. "But they must have sent for reinforcements by now. Even with their primitive weapons, a show of sheer numbers will ultimately overpower us."

"Do what you have to until the ship arrives," Medea said, her image winking out.

Dr. Morrow silently cursed her as the transmission ended. She should have sent a ship the first time he asked her. Now they would have to fight for their lives, and perhaps all of his work would be lost.

He stalked out of the room. Bursting through the door, he bellowed for technicians and workers to begin loading everything into the three skyfighters.

Sentry number one was still holding the serrated blade. The guard who had been watching him had been called forth to fight the attacking humans, and he was making his way to Dr.

Morrow's quarters with the intention of killing the one responsible for his friend's death.

Knowing a shortcut from one main corridor to the next, he took it. He was less likely to be seen, and it would save time.

At the end of the narrow passageway, he heard the clatter of a group of soldiers. He clung to the wall, waiting for them to pass.

One of them shouted. Had they spotted him? No, they stopped not five paces in front of him and stared at something in front of them. Their captain ordered them to aim their weapons and fire.

"Wait!" sentry number one cried.

It was over. Jack was sure of it. There was nowhere to run to get out of the line of fire. The guards were aiming their lasers at them. He hugged Sabrina hard and closed his eyes.

Suddenly a voice barked out something in the alien tongue.

A Visitor emerged from the shadows, holding one claw behind his back as if hiding something. The captain, who was about to signal those behind him to fire, hesitated.

The newcomer stepped forward, speaking softly. The captain leaned forward, straining to hear what he was saying. Suddenly the arm came out from behind the newcomer's back and struck down the captain with a blow of a serrated blade. Holding onto his neck and screaming in pain, the captain sank to the floor.

Leaping over the captain's body, the assailant chopped away at those guards nearest him. For a few seconds, they were so shocked they didn't know what to do. Four of them joined their captain before they began to fire, and three others were wounded or dead before a beam struck the attacker.

By that time, Jack and the others were on them, scooping up the lasers of fallen guards as they waded into the melee. The odds were only twelve to four now—five, counting the sentry, who was still hacking away while holding on to his wound.

Jack crouched and squeezed the trigger. A burst of blue light shot out and pierced the chest of the nearest Visitor. Marie dispatched another. Down to ten, two to one odds.

John Tiger charged headfirst at one who was leveling his weapon at Sabrina, knocking him to the floor and punching his face in. Two more came after him, and Sabrina fired at the nearest. The laser beam burned through him and struck the one behind him as well, bringing them both down.

"There's only seven of 'em left," Jack shouted, landing a well-placed kick in a Visitor's teeth. "We've got 'em outnumbered."

Sabrina and Marie shot two Visitors as they tried to get Jack in their sights. He was simply never in one place long enough for them to draw a bead on.

The sentry cut another one down, the victim of his blade screaming until his death throes ended seconds later.

The three remaining guards were firing wildly. A laser nicked John's ear, but the Visitor who fired it was dead in an instant.

The last two remaining soldiers tried to run, but now they had nowhere to go to get out of the line of fire.

Four laser beams fired almost at the same moment. It was impossible to tell who scored the last two shots of the skirmish.

The Visitor who had saved them with his surpise attack threw down his blade and sagged against a bulkhead. It was only then that Jack recognized him as the survivor of this evening's gladiatorial combat.

"Go now," the alien rasped. "I will die here."

"No, we can't leave you," said Jack. "Not after you helped us."

Through his pain, the alien stared at him quizzically. "You are a curious race," he said.

"Why?" Jack asked. "Because we help those who help us?"

"I did not do it for you, Terran. Dr. Morrow forced me to kill my friend, and I wish to avenge him. It was foolish of me to help you, but I thought you too would wish to kill Dr. Morrow. . . ."

The sentry quaked in Jack's arms, and then his body relaxed. Jack laid his body carefully on the floor. "You'll have your vengeance," he said softly.

Chapter 41

"Where *are* you, Donovan?" Ham Tyler said, looking up at the stars. His people were setting up makeshift barricades around him to protect themselves not only from laser fire, but also from tractor beams and a device that put people to sleep.

"Don't worry," Chris said. "He'll be here soon."

"Don't worry?" Ham glared at him in annoyance. "Stern and his girl friend are trapped in there, and so are Tiger and Marie."

"Getting kind of attached to that girl, Ham?"

"It doesn't matter how I feel. They're all crucial to this mission—if they're still alive."

"They're alive," Chris said, "to be used as bargaining chips."

"I hope you're right."

"Course I'm right, boss, and Mike Donovan will be here soon. I know you two don't always get along, considering how he blew the whistle on us in Central America, but you've got to admit he's always come through for us."

"Yeah." Ham looked up at the pristine white walls rising out of the mud. Occasionally a burst of laser fire would sear blue across the few hundred yards that separated the two forces. "What the hell are they doing in there, though? You'd think they would attack rather than let us dig in."

"They must have something up their sleeves besides scaly arms," Chris said.

"That's what I'm afraid of."

Their backs to the wall, the four fugitives crept through the alien compound. They came to a silent, deserted area that ended in a wall with a single door in its center.

"Let's try going in here," Jack said. He inserted the key and the door opened.

It was dark inside. Jack closed the door behind them and moved cautiously forward. Dim lights came on to guide his way, the others following close behind him.

It was a vast chamber. Their footsteps echoed as they examined huge vats and machines that looked like enormous meat grinders.

"What's this?" John asked.

"A meat-processing plant," Sabrina said. "This is where their victims were taken after they removed tissue samples."

"How do you know?" John didn't want to believe it.

"One of the scientists working here, Dr. Thorkel, told me about this place. He only found out about it recently himself."

"Billy . . ." Marie whispered. It was too horrible to think of.

John put his arm around her and led her away from the alien abattoir. Marie wept freely, but John found that the tears would not come, at least not until he had his revenge.

"I'm sorry," Sabrina said. "I didn't know."

Jack put a restraining hand on her arm. "Let them have a moment or two."

She nodded. It occurred to her that they might never find their way out of this maze without help. Dr. Thorkel had enjoyed considerable freedom until the past couple of days. He might know how to get out. Besides, she couldn't very well leave him here after he had tried to help her.

"Jack, I think I might know someone who can help us get out of here."

"Dr. Thorkel?"

"And they said you were just a big, dumb jock." She hugged him. "His quarters should be quite near this place."

At the far end of the abattoir, Jack inserted his crystal key in the wall. A door slid open and they found themselves looking out on a corridor with a row of doors facing them.

"That one down there on the end should be his," Sabrina said.

Jack beckoned for Marie and John to follow, and the four of them made their way to Dr. Thorkel's door. Their stealth paid off; they saw no sign of any Visitors.

Jack inserted the key. The opening door revealed a balding, middle-aged man wearing heavy spectacles, sitting at a desk.

The four fugitives slipped inside his room, and the door shut behind them.

"Dr. Thorkel," Sabrina said.

The man at the desk turned. All at once, Sabrina sensed there was something wrong. Dr. Thorkel's face looked at her, and yet . . .

"I knew you would come here," a rasping voice said, coming from Thorkel's mouth.

Panels opened on either side of them, and four red-clad Visitors sprang out, weapons pointed at them.

"Once a traitor . . . Jack said.

"On the contrary, Mr. Stern." Dr. Thorkel raised a hand and began to peel away his face. A few seconds later Dr. Morrow was revealed. "Dr. Thorkel turned out to be too courageous for his own good. I'm sure such stern stuff will make a delicious meal, if prepared properly."

"Then you've killed him," Sabrina said angrily.

"Crudely put, but accurate."

"You'll pay, you know," John Tiger said. "Help is on the way."

"You'll never get out of this swamp," Marie said with grim satisfaction.

"On the contrary, my dear woman." He flipped a switch on Dr. Thorkel's desk console, and a viewscreen lit up.

"This landing area is behind the inner wall of the experimental combat zone." Visitors were loading three skyfighters with scientific equipment. "Medea has sent a Mother Ship, which should be entering Earth's atmosphere very soon." Dr. Morrow clucked in satisfaction. "Any minute now, in fact. And you, Dr. Fontaine, will be accompanying me on the short journey to that Mother Ship."

"There won't be much room for these boys," Jack observed, nodding at the guards holding weapons on them. "Only a select few get to go, is that it, Dr. Morrow?"

Dr. Morrow's long tongue snaked nervously in and out of his mouth. "We will take as many as possible, and the skyfighters will return for those left behind."

"Those left behind will be dead," Jack said.

"They have the weapons to hold off the attack until the skyfighters return."

"Bull! There's another attack squadron on the way, led by experienced resistance fighters," John Tiger said. "And they're armed with lasers."

"Nonsense." Morrow's yellow, reptilian eyes glanced at his guards. "Surely you can see what they're doing. Trying to turn you against me."

Jack noted that there were only four guards. If they turned on Dr. Morrow, all well and good, and if they didn't, they still might be confused enough to lose a fight.

One of the guards said something in the alien tongue, and Dr. Morrow responded in kind. His angry response seemed to quell the guards' rebelliousness.

It's now or never, Jack thought.

The guards weren't looking at their prisoners. They were watching the confrontation between their master and their compatriot. The lasers were leveled at the four humans, but it would take an instant for the inattentive aliens to react. Jack dove into the nearest. The Visitor crumpled and collided with the one behind him.

John Tiger sprang into action, delivering a roundhouse punch to the jaw of the third guard.

The remaining guard began to fire wildly. Marie and Sabrina were both on him, and he toppled under their weight. His laser flew from his grasp, clattering on the plastic floor.

A moment later the four guards were disarmed. John held a laser on them while Jack and Marie searched them to make sure they didn't have any other weapons.

"That's enough!" Dr. Morrow hissed. "Stand over there."

Jack spun on his heels to see Sabrina with Dr. Morrow's scaly arm around her throat. His claw held a laser against her head.

"Did you think I was totally without defenses?" he sneered. "You and your friends underestimate me, Mr. Stern."

Jack lowered his laser pistol.

"Shoot him, Jack!" Sabrina cried.

"Go ahead," Dr. Morrow said. "See if you can kill me before I kill her."

"Come on, now," John said. "It's a standoff. Let her go."

"She will die before I let her go," Dr. Morrow rasped. "As that man has just said, it's a standoff. Go, and I will spare her life."

Jack moved a fraction of an inch toward them, and Dr. Morrow jammed the laser against Sabrina's temple. "Go!"

"Do as he says, man," John said. "At least we'll all be alive."

"But you don't understand," Jack said, never taking his eyes off Dr. Morrow and Sabrina. "You don't know what he wants to do to her."

John put his hand on Jack's shoulder. "I lost a brother to this creep," he said. "But I don't want to see this girl die, as much as I'd love to blast him right now."

Jack knew he was right, but he couldn't bear the thought of leaving Sabrina with this monster again.

"I command you to leave!" Dr. Morrow shrieked.

John and Marie gently led Jack to the door. As it slid shut behind them, Jack took one last look into Sabrina's brown eyes, seeing both love and despair in them.

An explosion rocked the corridor. Screams echoed as smoke billowed through the passageways.

"They're here!" Marie shouted joyously. "Our reinforcements are here!"

Chapter 42

An immense, circular shape hovered above the holographed trees. For a moment all combat ceased as everyone, human and Visitor alike, stopped to gape at the awesome spectacle above them. A Mother Ship.

But not for long. The quicksilver sound of laser fire again alternated with the popping of gunshots, the eerie ululation of the sleep ray was punctuated by rocket explosions, and the hum of antigravity disks underscored everything.

The resistance had the compound surrounded. They poured over the mud flat like ants, only to be repulsed by the tractor beam. The swamp buzzed with the sound of hydroplanes and the droning of air boats. From the walls and towers, bright blue death rained down, but the resistance fought on, hour after hour, cheering whenever a sentry was picked off the walls or towers and silently mourning when they lost one of their own.

"Haven't been able to penetrate the walls yet," Ham Tyler shouted into a walkie-talkie. "They're seamless—impossible to tell where the entrances are."

"They can't hold out forever," Mike Donovan's voice crackled. Mike was inside the skyfighter Willie had piloted

from Los Angeles. They were waiting for Dr. Morrow to try
and make his escape. The shuttle craft was hidden just far
enough away from the compound so it couldn't be spotted.
That was going to be their final surprise. Julie and Elias were
with him and Willie.

Directing the battle, Ham ordered a rocket launcher to fire
straight at the center of the wall. The missile *shushed* across
the mud flat, exploded thunderously on impact, and left not a
single mark on the gleaming, white surface.

Ham noticed that the disk riders were retreating, floating
behind the compound's walls. Maybe he could still nail one or
two more.

"Lob one over the top!" he shouted through the din. A
rocket was fired, but it exploded a few yards over the towers.
Through a pair of binoculars, Ham saw a rippling force field
covering the entire compound, distorting the image of the
sentries as they fired their lasers down at his people.

A beam hit the gas tank of an air boat. As it blew up, the
bodies of its passengers flew through the air. Ham was furious
to think there was no way to shoot the sentries now that the
force field was up.

"There's gotta be a way to get in there." Ham knew he was
grasping at straws, but he had to try. "Maybe that field won't
stay up for long—it may take too much power."

"Maybe," Chris said, "and maybe not."

"What else can we do?" Ham turned to the rocket man
again, but before he could order another brace to be fired
fruitlessly at the wall, something happened.

A vertical line appeared right in the middle of the wall. It
was about eight feet high from top to bottom. It opened and
there stood Jack Stern, Marie Whitley, and John Tiger, holding
off pursuing Visitors with laser pistols.

Stern glanced over his shoulder between shots and waved
the resistance fighters on.

"What are you waiting for?" Ham bellowed. "Let's go!"

A flood of resistance fighters swept out from behind
barricades and funneled through the open entrance into the

compound. The Visitors chasing Jack and the others turned tail and ran as soon as they saw them coming.

Ham and Chris ran to the wall, ducking enemy fire as they went. As he approached Stern, Ham saw that the man was on the verge of collapse. His face was drawn and haggard, his shirt torn open, blood caked on his shoulder.

"You look like hell," Ham said. "Come with me."

"They've got Sabrina," Jack said. "I have to go back for her."

"She won't be in there by the time you . . ." Ham didn't have to finish. The whine of skyfighter engines announced the departure of Dr. Morrow and his chosen few survivors.

"Sabrina!" Jack cried as the first skyfighter rose over the white towers.

"We might still be able to catch them," Ham said. "Come on, hurry."

Dodging the laser fire from the walls, they sprinted across the mud flats. Ham was amazed that Jack not only kept up, he actually had to slow his pace and wait for the others. A second skyfighter rose over the compound like an albino vulture.

"This way," Ham said, leading them to a path cut through dense undergrowth. Ahead, they heard the whine of engines cutting in.

They were there in minutes. Suddenly they were in an area where the vegetation was cut back for seventy feet. Ensconced in the secluded clearing was a skyfighter.

A hatch opened in its side, and they all clambered aboard— Jack, Chris, Ham, Marie, and John.

On the viewscreen, the third and last skyfighter rose from the compound.

"Think you can catch it, Donovan?" Ham asked.

"We'll see what we can do," Mike Donovan told him. At the controls was Willie. Elias Taylor stood by, and Julie Parrish sat at one of the big laser cannons. "Welcome aboard," she said.

The shuttle craft lifted off the ground. The moment it cleared the treetops, Willie touched a light on the console and they shot forward so rapidly it took their breath away.

The first two alien-directed skyfighters had turned and rocketed skyward toward the looming Mother Ship. The third was just in the process of turning over the compound when Julie got it in her sights. She fired a broadside and scored a direct hit on the starboard side.

A split second later, the wounded skyfighter shot off over the swamp, pointed away from the Mother Ship.

"I hoped they'd do that," Julie said. "They aren't willing to wait around long enough for us to get off another shot."

Willie piloted the shuttle craft on a direct pursuit course, the swamp racing by beneath them.

"They're hoping to outrun us," Mike Donovan said, "or lose us. But they're wounded, not us."

Their prey eluded them, moving closer to the ground, wending its way dangerously between trees. Now Mike manned the other cannon.

"Grace yourselves," Willie said.

"What?" everyone asked in unison.

"He meant, 'Brace yourselves,'" Mike shouted, but it was too late. They were slammed against the bulkheads as Willie banked the skyfighter hard.

As they veered past the enemy ship, Mike got off a series of shots with the laser cannon.

Like a crimson flower, the flaming explosion opened from inside the wounded skyfighter and grew, layer after flaming layer. Debris was thrown out, spinning and smoking over the swamp, until it splashed sizzling into the water.

"Now lets go after the rest," Elias said.

Willie banked the shuttle craft again, its nose pointed toward the sky. He ran his fingers over the console, and they were hurled upward at a tremendous velocity.

Chapter 43

The Mother Ship was immense, larger than any structure on earth. To see such a machine floating in the sky was awesome enough, but approaching it was even more startling. Jack kept thinking that they were going to dock with it at any second, but the Mother Ship proved to be much farther away—and consequently much larger—than he imagined.

Willie had communicated with it, claiming to be the pilot of the demolished skyfighter and explaining that they had been chased but the enemy vessel had been destroyed in the ensuing dogfight.

"Think they bought it?" Mike asked.

Willie shrugged. "Perhaps."

"They could be leading us on, couldn't they?" Ham said. "Waiting for us to get aboard before they let on they know who we are."

"Could be," Mike agreed.

"Do you think we should turn back?" Willie asked.

Everyone aboard the shuttle craft did a double take.

"Turn back?" Jack said. "Listen, I don't know if it means anything to you, but someone I love is aboard that ship."

Mike and Julie took Jack aside. "He lost somebody he loved," Julie said. "That's one of the reasons he's with us today."

Jack was ashamed. "I'm sorry," he said to Willie. "It's just that . . ."

Willie looked sad as he sat at the controls. "I understand, my friend. We must go on."

"There's no turning back now anyway," Mike said. The Mother Ship's tractor beam was drawing them in. Willie no longer had command of the skyfighter.

The last thing Jack saw before they entered the immense docking bay was the coast of Florida, the streets of Miami and Fort Lauderdale far below, the green and yellow squares of farmland to the west melting into the lush green of the Everglades.

And then they were inside the monstrous Mother Ship. The shuttle craft settled to the floor, the last in a neat row of alien vessels.

"Put these on," Mike said, watching the technicians through the viewscreen. He handed them swatches of red material. When unfolded, they turned out to be Visitor uniforms. Billed caps and dark glasses completed their disguises.

"The skyfighter next door just unloaded a few lizards," Chris said. "Your girlfriend wasn't with them."

"She must have been on the first one," Ham said. "She could be anywhere on this big mother by now."

"Find Morrow," Jack said, "and you'll find Sabrina. Let's go for it."

"Take it easy," Mike said. "I've been aboard these ships before. We'll never find anybody if we come out blasting. Just climb out and act like you belong here. Even though you won't know where you're going, act like you do. Once we get into the ship's infrastructure, we can play duck and run, but here we're stationary targets. Got it?"

Jack liked this guy. There was a tough, no-nonsense air about him that inspired confidence. Their chances were slim, but if anyone could pull it off, it was this group.

"All right," Jack said, seeing the last of the Visitors leave the skyfighter while the workers readied themselves to refuel the vessel they were in. "Let's go."

The hatch swung open and Willie hopped out first. Jack handed him a piece of equipment as calmly as possible and followed. Then came Marie, John, Ham, Julie, Elias, and Chris. When they were all on the landing bay floor, Mike swung his lithe body out of the hatch and walked behind them.

The Visitor techs handled huge hoses, steam spraying from their nozzles, as they went to work. None of them paid much attention to the group making its way to the nearest exit. They were, as far as the technicians were concerned, just the survivors of a failed mission on Earth.

Mike glanced from side to side as inconspicuously as he could. He didn't see a single green face. Everyone was wearing human makeup, perhaps in anticipation of some covert operation on the planet's surface.

He felt a hand on his shoulder. Turning, he faced a Visitor who spoke to him in the alien language. Mike felt a tight knot of fear rise in his guts. He had no idea what this lizard was saying, and his ignorance was going to become obvious in a moment.

The Visitor repeated his rasping question. Desperate, Mike pointed to his mouth and made dumb noises, making his moans and groans as scratchy as his throat could bear.

Willie stepped in, speaking quietly to the curious alien. He then grabbed Mike's elbow and led him away.

As soon as they were out of earshot, Willie said, "He was asking after a friend who was a sentry at the compound."

"What did you tell him?"

"That his friend was left behind."

"Do you think it worked?" Mike asked.

"I don't know," Willie replied. "Keep walking."

Mike felt the tech's eyes boring into his back. "He's still watching us, isn't he?"

"Yes, he—"

A bloodcurdling shout interrupted Willie's answer. Jack

looked back to see the tech pointing at them, still shouting. Visitors were dropping hoses and staring at them.

"Run!" Mike yelled.

They bolted for the exit, footsteps clattering behind them and the susurrating sound of laser fire over their heads.

Chapter 44

Jack spun and pulled out his laser pistol. He saw Mike and Willie firing at the oncoming horde of techs, barely slowing them down even when bodies rolled in front of them.

"Let's get out of here!" Ham bellowed from inside the passageway. Elias and the others were right behind him.

They sprinted to the nearest adjoining corridor and turned left. At the next juncture, they made a right, then another left. Mike hoped to lose the techs in the maze of passageways, at least for the moment. The only chance they had was to make it to the heart of the ship, the command center, before the entire crew was alerted to their presence.

"We've got to split up!" he shouted. If they could confuse those pursuing them, even for a little while, he might just get to the command center. Otherwise, the humans were nothing but rats in a trap. It was up to Mike to do the job; he was the only one who could find the command center quickly enough.

He darted down a narrow passageway. Two Visitors were running toward him. He shot them down before they had a chance to level their lasers at him.

Jumping over their smoking bodies, Mike made another left turn, trusting in his usually unerring sense of direction to get him to the ship's center. He came to an intersection of four corridors. Which way now?

"Mike!"

He leaped out of the way as a Visitor pounced from above. Before the alien hit the floor, a laser beam had burned through his stomach.

Julie ran to help Mike up.

"Good shot," he said.

She hugged him. "Those long legs of yours are hard to keep up with."

They were off and running again, dodging down corridor after corridor, often having to fight their way through, backtracking, then heading back the way Mike sensed they must go if they were to make it.

Suddenly they confronted a vertical cylinder where the corridors all ended like the inner spokes of a wheel.

"This is it," Mike breathed.

Julie nodded, huffing and puffing next to him.

A door opened, startling them.

"Quick!" Mike jerked the grating off an air vent and lifted Julie up so she could crawl inside. He followed, replacing the vent just as doors slid open all around the command center.

Dozens of Visitors streamed out of each door, drawing their lasers as they ran down the corridors nearest them. Several passed directly below Mike and Julie.

The moment the last of them was out of earshot, Mike kicked the grating off and jumped down. The closest door was closing from the top. It was already halfway down.

He dashed toward it, diving and rolling under with only inches to spare. He came up in a crouch on the inside, pointing his laser at the startled Visitors gathered around their consoles.

"Stand over there," he commanded them, gesturing with the barrel of the laser.

They did as he told them.

"Now open the door and leave it open."

A Visitor inserted a crystal key in a slot next to the door, and the door slid up.

"Julie," he called, "it's all right. Come on in."

Julie entered, laser at the ready.

"Now," Mike said, "set the command to blow this thing to atoms."

The Visitors looked at him in horror, their artificial eyes widening convincingly. "We will all die," one of them finally managed to say.

"It will take a little while for the delayed command to take effect," Mike told him. "We should have enough time to reach the skyfighters."

"But your planet is getting farther away every nanosecond," a voice said from behind them.

Mike and Julie both turned at the same moment. A dark-haired woman looked at them through frightened eyes. Around her neck was the scaly green arm of a Visitor who wore no makeup. At the end of the Visitor's other arm was a claw clutching a laser whose barrel was pressed against the woman's head.

"We wouldn't want to be too close to Earth when we detonate this thing, would we?" Mike asked coolly.

"If you are too far away," Dr. Morrow said, "the skyfighters will not be able to carry you back to your planet."

"It's a chance we'll have to take," Julie said.

"Ah," Dr. Morrow sighed. "But Dr. Fontaine will have no chance. She will die here where we stand."

"Then *you'll* die," Mike promised.

"Then we'll *all* die." Dr. Morrow seemed pleased by this little game of one-upmanship he was playing. "Enough, Mr. Donovan. Throw down your weapons or I will kill her right now."

Mike and Julie hesitated.

"Now!" Dr. Morrow shrieked.

They threw down their lasers, defeated by Dr. Morrow's ruthlessness.

"You have lost, Mr. Donovan and Dr. Parrish," Dr. Morrow gloated. "You have not only lost the battle, but the entire war."

"We'll see about that," Julie said. "It's not over yet."

"But it is over. Dr. Fontaine and I are going to conceive a child the equal of Elizabeth, a child which I will personally train to unleash its powers against your kind, destroying you all."

"The child can never hold that kind of power without the *Preta-na-ma*," Mike said, "and the *Preta-na-ma* teaches peace."

"You mistakenly believe that the ancient secrets can only be applied traditionally," Dr. Morrow said. "It is the work of the scientist to find new ways to accomplish great things."

"Is it the work of a scientist to warp a child's mind?" Julie asked. "To turn a great philosophy into an instrument of hate? I think you're mistaken, Dr. Morrow."

"No, *you're* mistaken, and you're beaten," he taunted. "If only you had possessed enough foresight to close this door behind you." He shoved Sabrina forward a step across the threshold. "But you didn't do that, did you?"

"Neither did you." A powerful hand shot out and grabbed Dr. Morrow's wrist in a viselike grip. The laser pistol clattered to the floor as Dr. Morrow gasped and released Sabrina.

Jack Stern lifted him bodily off the floor, slamming him against the bulkhead with one hand. He still clutched Dr. Morrow's wrist, and the sound of crunching bones was clearly audible.

"Their weapons!" Dr. Morrow screamed. "Get their weapons!"

But the command center crew weren't fast enough. Mike darted after the two lasers he and Julie had dropped a few moments ago.

Dr. Morrow was still pinned against the bulkhead, Jack's left hand encircling his throat. He gagged and sputtered, his yellow eyes bulging.

Everyone, human and Visitor alike, watched in silence. It was as though a ritual were being performed that could not be interrupted. The ritual of revenge.

Green fluid bubbled out of Dr. Morrow's jaws, dribbling onto Jack's hand. The scaly mouth opened wide, revealing the spiky teeth within. Another gout of green poured out, and then the head slumped, lolling to one side.

Dr. Morrow was dead.

Chapter 45

"Set the detonator," Mike demanded.

"The explosion will be enough to destroy your world," one of the Visitors said fearfully.

"You heard what your boss said before he died—we're moving away from Earth rapidly."

"But even so, it may not be far enough."

"I think it will be."

"If it is, you will never be able to get back to Earth."

"That's a chance we'll have to take, isn't it? Now, do it."

The Visitor stretched a claw toward the command console and hesitated.

Mike aimed the laser right between his eyes. "Do it!"

The Visitor did it, computer graphics illustrating the process as he punched in the secret code that would turn the ship into a hydrogen bomb powerful enough to destroy the entire earth.

At last he looked up from the console. "It's done," he rasped.

Mike pushed him ahead out the door. Jack stood over the corpse of Dr. Morrow, flexing and unflexing his mighty hands. Sabrina embraced him, gently leading him away by one arm.

Julie took the other, and they followed Mike and his hostage, leaving the rest of the command center crew gawking behind them.

Outside the door they found Willie, Ham, Chris, Marie, Elias, and John waiting for them, weapons in hands.

"Come on," Mike said. "This thing's gonna blow in a few minutes."

"You did it," Ham said, his usual cynicism completely absent. "You really did it, didn't you, Mike?"

"Maybe. We still have to get a skyfighter. Our friend here is the ship's engineer, I believe." Mike poked the back of the Visitor's skull with his laser. "I'm betting they won't want him to die."

He glanced back into the command center. "You want to die in space?" he shouted at the crew. "Go on."

They ran out and scrambled down the nearest corridor.

"There's no turning back now," Chris said. "If they could have bollixed that detonation code, they would have."

They didn't run through the Mother Ship's passageways. Instead, they walked behind Mike and their prisoner single file, straight into a spacious, dark area milling with Visitors.

"Don't say a word," Mike instructed the hostage, "or you'll be the first to die."

They stepped into the enclosure. "Let us go and we won't kill your engineer," Mike said in a clear, authoritative tone. "We only want to go back to our planet."

As if in a motion-picture freeze frame, the crowd stopped virtually all movement and fell silent.

"Just let us go to the docking bay without any trouble, and we'll borrow a skyfighter. If you do that, he will live. If you attack us, I'll be forced to kill him."

"Gather around Mike," Ham said to the others. They formed a rough circle around him and the engineer, all of them moving as one through the enclosure.

They passed so close to the resentful Visitors that they could hear the reptilian creatures breathing. Slowly the corridor on the far side of the big chamber drew nearer.

Jack felt sweat standing out on his forehead and running

down his temples and cheeks. A few days ago he'd been in Miami, working out with his teammates—and now he was running interference against creatures who were trying to conquer Earth.

They were almost there. Once they got to that corridor, it would be a lot more difficult for the Visitors to stop them. They would reach a bottleneck at the narrow passage if they gave chase.

Jack was facing backward, sweaty hand on his laser. Julie and Sabrina—his darling Sabrina—were on either side of him. For the first time he began to think they could make it.

The wailing of a demon echoed through the enclosure, reverberating through the corridor and deafening them.

"What the hell is that?" Jack yelled over the din.

The startled faces of the Visitors told him what it was: an alarm warning of the imminent destruction of the Mother Ship.

Shrill cries, hisses, and rasped oaths filled the enclosure. A blue beam streaked through the faint light within, barely missing Marie's head.

Mike shoved the engineer out of the way. "Run!" he bellowed.

His companions-in-arms were way ahead of him. They dashed down the dark corridor, their way lit by the laser beams of their enemies.

Chapter 46

Somehow they made it to the docking bay without losing anyone. By this time the entire ship was in a state of panic, the Visitors either running around in confusion or readying the skyfighters for flight.

Mike held up his hand at the mouth of the corridor overlooking the docking bay. "Wait until they get one fueled," he said. "Just when they're ready to board, we'll make a break for it. If we can fight our way through this crowd, we've got a chance."

They all waited, knowing that a chance was only a slim one. One of the skyfighters lifted off the bay floor as the enormous hatch opened to let it out into the starlit blackness.

Bulky hoses were clamped to the bottom of the next skyfighter in line. Fights were breaking out on the docking bay floor as everyone tried to position himself to board the departing craft.

Somehow the techs managed to keep the rabble from storming the skyfighter. Perhaps they sensed that their only chance for survival depended on a few moments' patience.

Those few moments were enough for the resistance fighters

to race across the mobbed floor to the newly fueled skyfighter. Flicking tongues and widened, yellow eyes rushed past as they sprinted. Those who saw them cried shrilly, but their voices were lost amid the chaos.

They only had a few more yards to go when the hatch opened and the technicians allowed the first few to board the skyfighter. Shoving Visitors out of the way, Jack was the first of the resistance fighters to reach the ramp. He turned to pull Sabrina up beside him.

"Stop them!" a strident, reptilian voice rasped.

Jack picked a Visitor up over his head and hurled him into the crowd as his friends clambered aboard. The body knocked half a dozen Visitors to the floor, clearing the ramp.

All the while the hideous howl of the siren sounded a continuous note of doom in the background.

Jack pulled the ramp up with his powerful arms, shutting out that dreadful sound forever. Willie was at the console, and the skyfighter lifted off the docking bay floor. As Willie turned the skyfighter toward the stars, Jack saw the terrified Visitors below them, claws raised in enraged frustration.

The huge hangar door of the docking bay began to close.

"Willie . . ." Mike tried to stay calm.

Willie ran his hand over the console. The doorway narrowed. All aboard the skyfighter watched with fascinated dread.

The engines pulsed, and they hurtled through the closing bay door with only centimeters to spare.

"Stern!" Ham shouted. "Fire that laser cannon at the panel next to the docking bay door."

Jack jumped into a swiveling chair suspended above the floor in the tail of the skyfighter. He glanced at the controls, not consciously knowing what to do. And yet, as soon as he put his hands on the grips, he squeezed the firing mechanism and watched the blazing twin beams sear the curved shell of the Mother Ship. The docking bay door began to reopen.

He kept firing until he could control his shots. Then he lined up the panel, which was diminishing to a tiny rectangle as the skyfighter gained speed. The nose of another skyfighter appeared in the opening door.

The panel in the Mother Ship was sliced open in a shower of sparks. A flaming jet licked silently outward, and the door convulsed. The emerging skyfighter, its pilot anticipating the timing of the door, collided with its solid edges and exploded.

The resistance fighters cheered and hugged each other. But it wasn't over yet.

"How much time do we have before the Mother Ship blows?" Julie asked.

"One minute," Willie said, never taking his gaze off the console. "Perhaps two."

"The rest of them will never get off that ship, but one skyfighter got out before us."

Willie nodded. A moment later, their ship veered off, affording them a breathtaking view of Earth's rising blue-white curve.

A tiny, gleaming mote over the azimuth was the refugee skyfighter.

"They don't know we're after them," Mike said. "Can you come up under them, Willie?"

The alien nodded, turning on a burst of speed. "We are close enough to your world to take advantage of the gravity well," he said, "but far enough away to maneuver quickly, our antigravity engines playing against the tidal forces."

Plummeting toward Earth, they gained quickly on the unsuspecting passengers of the other skyfighter. Willie pointed the nose up as Mike seated himself at the other laser cannon.

"Fire!" he shouted as the belly of the skyfighter came across their sights.

Jack and Mike both fired at the same instant. Blue flame danced along the skyfighter's hull, but she didn't explode. Instead, she banked and hurtled off the way she had come.

"Let's go after her," John Tiger said, excited in the heat of battle.

"You got it!" Mike yelled. "Let's go, Willie!"

The wounded skyfighter zigzagged through space, the moon's cratered face peering down at her. Willie observed her course on his console screen, doing his best to duplicate its serpentine trajectory.

They gained on it, but suddenly the crippled skyfighter banked to the right and shot off straight toward the Mother Ship.

"They're slowing down," Jack said. "We can catch 'em."

"Come on," Elias hollered. "Go for it, Willie."

"No!" cried Willie.

Their skyfighter banked, Willie frantically working his hands over the console. Frustrated cries rose from the resistance fighters.

And then they saw the wisdom in what Willie had done.

Jagged lines of pure white light appeared in the curve of the Mother Ship's fuselage. They grew into abstract blots of brilliance and joined, the hurtling debris unable to outrun the heat.

Earth and moon were lost in the blinding brilliance. Ahead, a tiny fleck of black showed against the mushrooming effulgence. It was the crippled skyfighter, banking, trying to turn around.

It was absorbed into the omnipresent light.

The light reached out past where the wounded skyfighter had been, stretching to cross the emptiness of space and take the second skyfighter—the one they were in.

"No!" Marie cried.

"God help us," Jack prayed.

"At least we got them first," Ham said.

The burning light that filled the emptiness steadied, no longer increasing.

They held their breath.

And waited.

The light remained . . . but it began to fade.

None of them moved as it slowly diminished, receding gradually into the darkness of space, leaving nothing in its wake.

As if from a trance, they were roused by a crackling, female voice. The image of Medea, the fleet commander, appeared in their midst. She was transmitting from her Mother Ship based beyond the moon.

"Why doesn't anyone aboard answer?" she demanded angrily.

"Can you patch us in to that transmission, Willie?" Mike asked.

Medea's eyes widened as she saw Mike Donovan standing before her. "Dr. Morrow?" she said, enraged. "What is this?"

"Dr. Morrow is dead," Mike told her. "The ship has been destroyed and all of his secrets with it. Nice try, but you lose again."

Medea's nostrils flared. Her reptilian nature seemed to show through the beautiful human face she wore. She slammed her palm down, and the transmission ended.

As his friends began to cheer, Mike held up a restraining hand. "Let's see if we make it home before we start partying."

Willie pointed the skyfighter toward the sunlit side of Earth. As soon as they were close enough, he cut the engines and let Earth's gravity do the work.

They sank toward the luxurious white clouds and the cerulean oceans, coasting all the way home.

Chapter 47

Jack stood watching the bonfire burn, one arm in a sling and the other around Sabrina's waist. She leaned her head on his shoulder as the Indians danced and laughed with the other resistance fighters, celebrating their victory against a common enemy.

Mike, Julie, Elias, and Willie had returned to the West Coast. Jack had been sorry to see them go, but everyone else was here tonight. John Tiger and Marie approached them, walking around from the other side of the bonfire. They were dressed in the traditional bright colors and feathers of their people.

"I don't know how to thank you," Sabrina said to them.

"You don't owe us any thanks," John replied, holding up his hand palm outward. "Marie and I both lost someone we loved. It was tough, but I think we both learned something."

"What was that?"

They turned to see Ham and Chris approaching, drinks in their hands. "What did you learn?" Ham asked.

"That sometimes we have to work together. Corny, but it's true."

"That," Ham said, holding out a bottle as a peace offering, "was what I tried to tell you when we first got here."

John said nothing for a moment, staring at Ham as if sizing him up. "Yeah, maybe you did," he said, slowly breaking into a grin. "It wasn't that I didn't dig your message, it's just that people like you have always given us plenty to be suspicious of."

"Let's talk about that some other time." Ham offered the bottle again.

John smiled and accepted it, taking a healthy swig and making a face. "What is that stuff?" he gasped.

Ham looked slyly at Chris, and then at Jack and Sabrina. "Lizard oil," he said.

They all laughed. Tonight they would have a good time, but every one of them knew that it wasn't the end of the war. Mike and Julie's absence underscored that fact.

But until the Visitors returned, they had lives to enjoy, and that was something they hadn't been able to do over the past few days.

"Jack?" Ham offered the bottle.

"No, thanks. We're gonna take a little walk."

"Not toward the compound," Marie said. "There's a whole team of exobiologists going through what the Visitors left behind over there."

Sabrina smiled at her. "You're right, Marie. It's probably way too crowded there."

"Have fun," John said.

Jack and Sabrina said they would, and walked away hand in hand.